UP NEXT >>>

on **Sports Illustrated KIDS**

:02 SPORTS ZONE SPECIAL REPORT

:04 FEATURE PRESENTATION:

POINT-BLANK PAINTBALL

FOLLOWED BY:

:50 SPORTS ZONE POSTGAME RECAP

:51 SPORTS ZONE POSTGAME EXTRA

:52 SI KIDS INFO CENTER

✔ P9-AGU-755

TWIN SIBLINGS NOAH AND PETER WILL COMPETE FOR ONE SPOT ON THE ROYALS' ELIT **SIK** TICKER

SPORTS ZONE

SPECIAL REPORT

PNT
PAINTBALL

FBL
FOOTBALL

SKT
SKATEBOARDING

BSL
BASEBALL

BBL
BASKETBALL

TALENTED TWINS TO COMPETE FOR SOLE SPOT ON TOP TEAM!

PETER ECCLESTON

STATS:
ROLE: POINTMAN
AGE: 14
COLORS: BLUE AND SILVER

BIO: Peter Eccleston is super-smart and ultra-organized on — and off — the paintball course. He prefers to play it cool and plan ahead, setting traps and preparing ambushes to keep his opponents off-guard.

NOAH ECCLESTON

STATS:
ROLE: MARKSMAN
AGE: 14
COLORS: ORANGE AND GREEN

BIO: Noah Eccleston is as playful and rebellious as they come. Only his twin brother, Peter, can get this class clown to quit joking around and stay serious. While Peter prefers to hang back and pick off opponents one by one, trigger-happy Noah would rather charge forward and open fire on the competition.

Sports Illustrated KIDS

UP NEXT: POINT-BLANK PAINTBALL

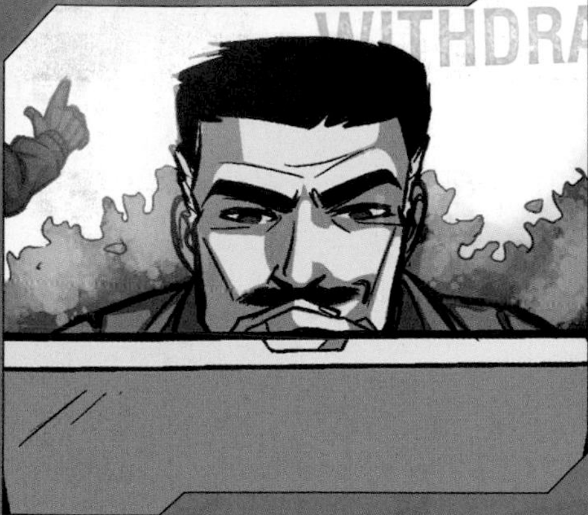

JOSEPH ECCLESTON

BIO: Joseph Eccleston is the father of Peter and Noah. A successful businessman, Mr. Eccleston believes that in life, you can only count on yourself. He puts a lot of pressure on his sons to succeed, and insists they compete with each other in everything.

BLZ vs BRS 3-1
TGR vs RDR 33-32
EAG vs BAN 14-7
SPA vs WLD 4-3
BAN vs RDR 21-15
RZR vs LIG

JOHN PATTERSON

TEAM: ROYALS **AGE:** 37 **ROLE:** COACH

BIO: Coach Patterson is a three-time state paintball champion. He has a reputation for turning paintball rookies into pros.

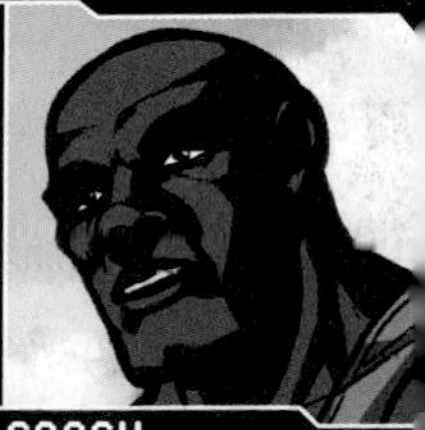

COACH

SAM "KING" LIONEL

TEAM: ROYALS **AGE:** 15 **ROLE:** CO-CAPTAIN

BIO: A gifted sharpshooter, King rarely misses the mark. The Royals count on him to remain calm even under heavy enemy fire.

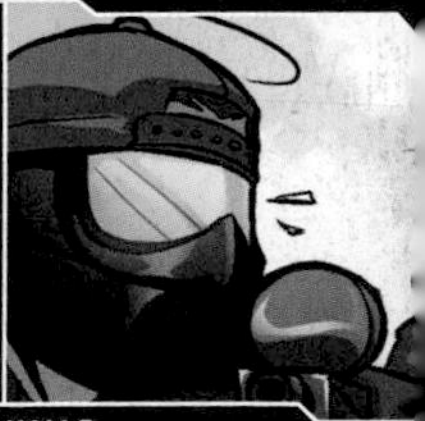

KING

CORA "QUEEN" RAMIREZ

TEAM: ROYALS **AGE:** 14 **ROLE:** CO-CAPTAIN

BIO: Cora "Queen" Ramirez is the brains behind the Royals. She's a gifted strategist and a natural born leader.

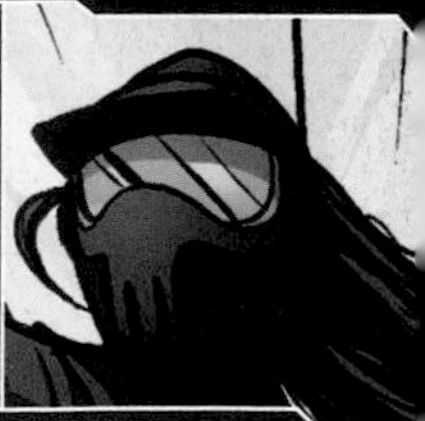

QUEEN

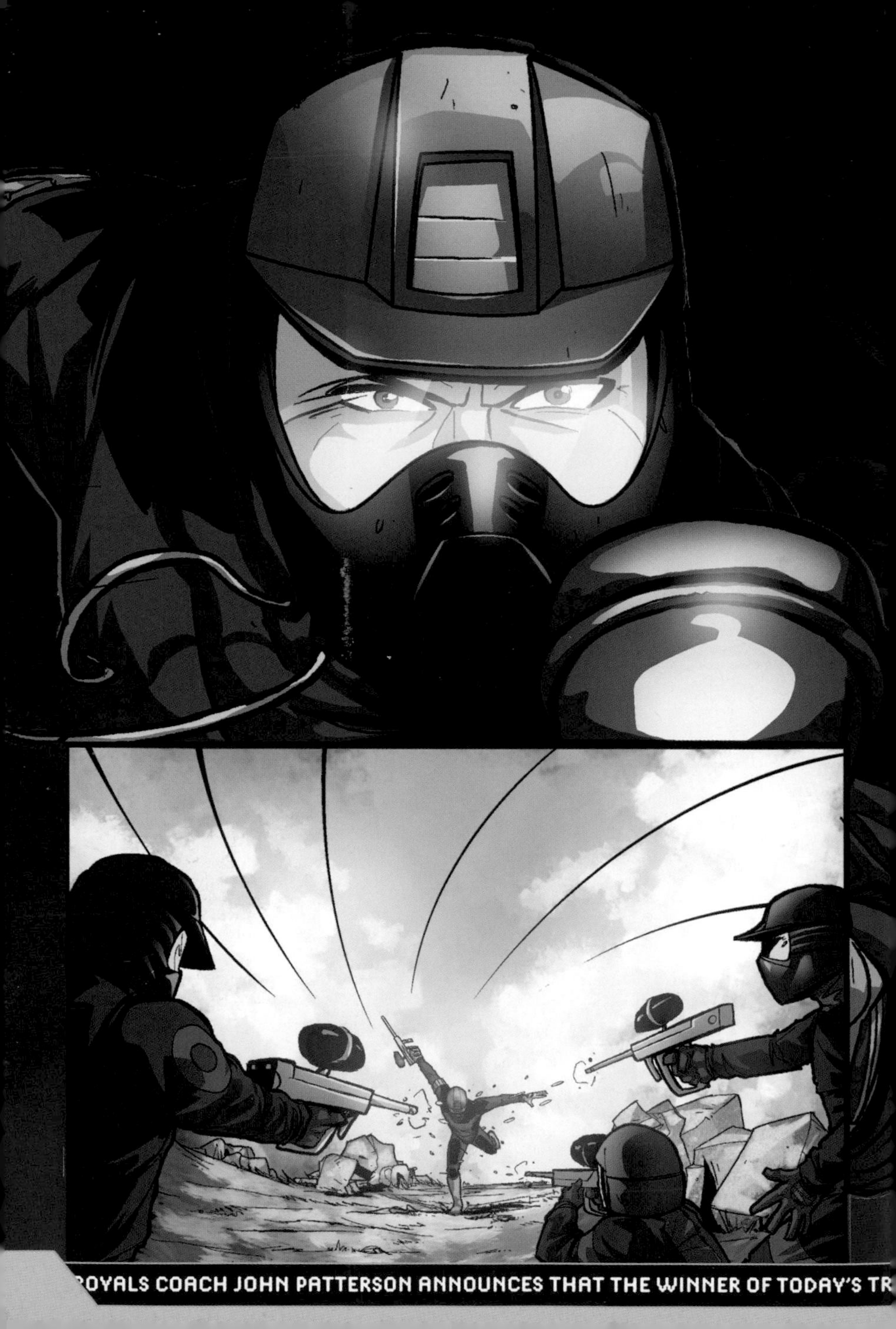
ROYALS COACH JOHN PATTERSON ANNOUNCES THAT THE WINNER OF TODAY'S TR

Sports Illustrated KIDS

PRESENTS

POINT-BLANK PAINTBALL

A PRODUCTION OF

STONE ARCH BOOKS
a capstone imprint

written by Scott Ciencin
illustrated by Jesus Aburto
colored by Fares Maese
Andres Esparza

designed and directed by Bob Lentz
edited by Sean Tulien
creative direction by Heather Kindseth
editorial direction by Michael Dahl

Sports Illustrated Kids *Point-Blank Paintball* is published by Stone Arch Books,
1710 Roe Crest Drive, North Mankato, Minnesota 56003.
www.capstonepub.com

Summary: Peter and Noah Eccleston are identical twins, so it's no surprise they make the perfect paintball teammates. But when Coach Patterson offers them a chance to compete for a single spot on his elite paintball team, the brothers turn on each other. With markers blazing, the twins cut down the competition with ease. But when they finally face each other for a point-blank shootout, who will be the first to pull the trigger?

Cataloging-in-Publication Data is available on the Library of Congress website.

ISBN 978-1-4342-1914-5 (library binding)
ISBN 978-1-4342-2293-0 (paperback)
ISBN 978-1-4342-4950-0 (e-book)

Printed in the United States 4165

L BE A STARTER IN SATURDAY'S TELEVISED STATE CHAMPIONSHIP MATC SIK TICKER

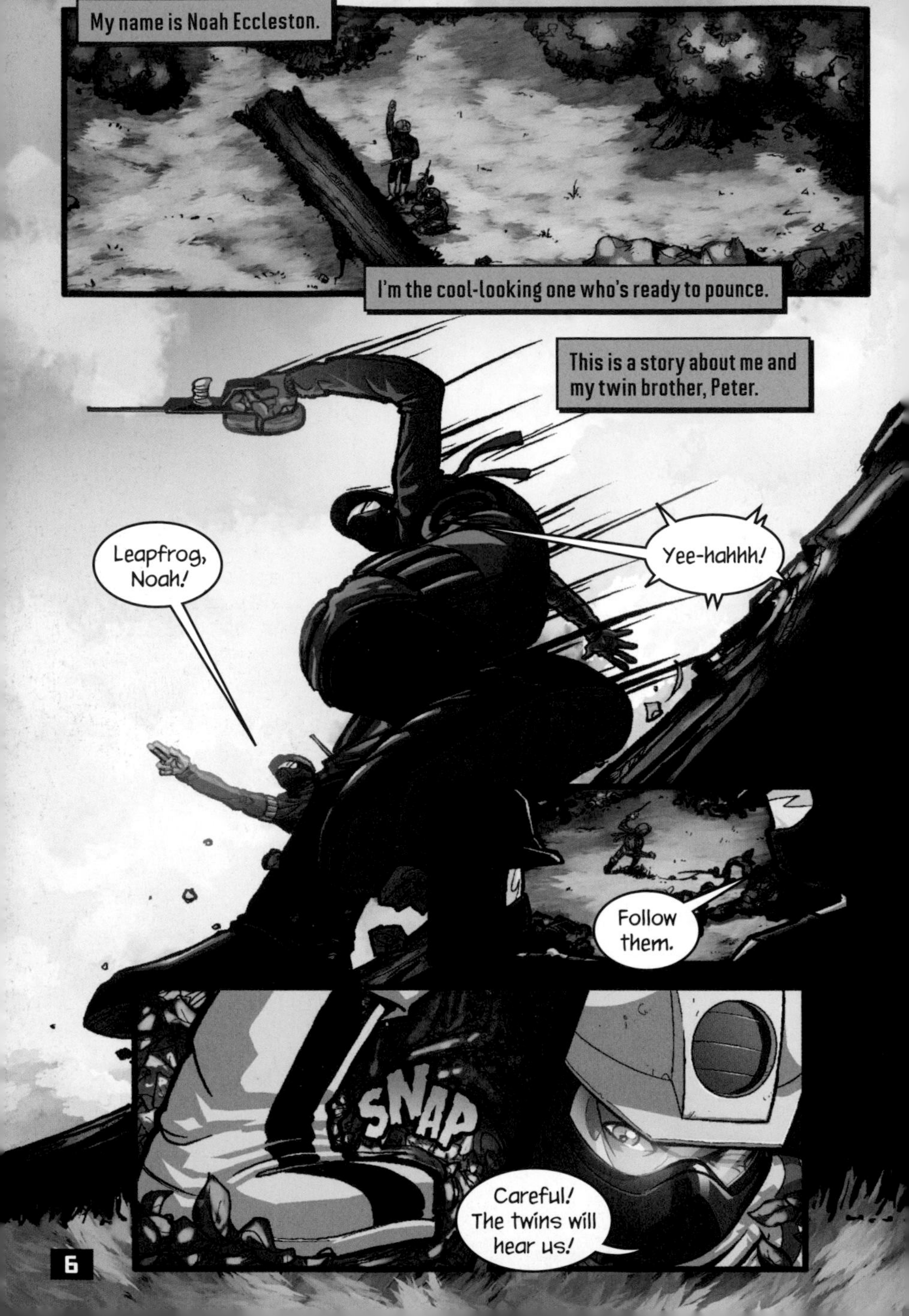

My name is Noah Eccleston.
I'm the cool-looking one who's ready to pounce.
This is a story about me and my twin brother, Peter.
Leapfrog, Noah!
Yee-hahhh!
Follow them.
SNAP
Careful! The twins will hear us!

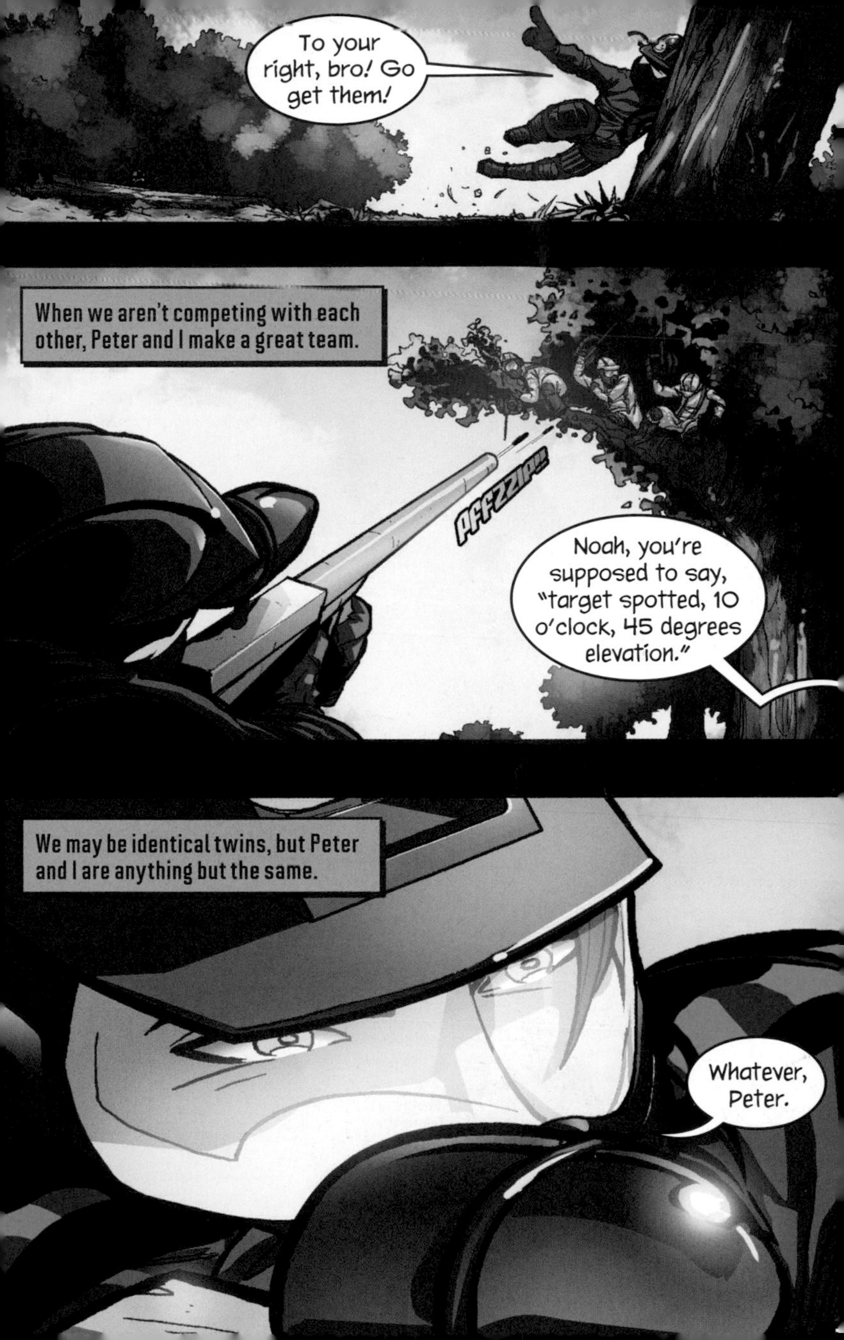

To your right, bro! Go get them!
When we aren't competing with each other, Peter and I make a great team.
PFFZZIP!!
Noah, you're supposed to say, "target spotted, 10 o'clock, 45 degrees elevation."
We may be identical twins, but Peter and I are anything but the same.
Whatever, Peter.

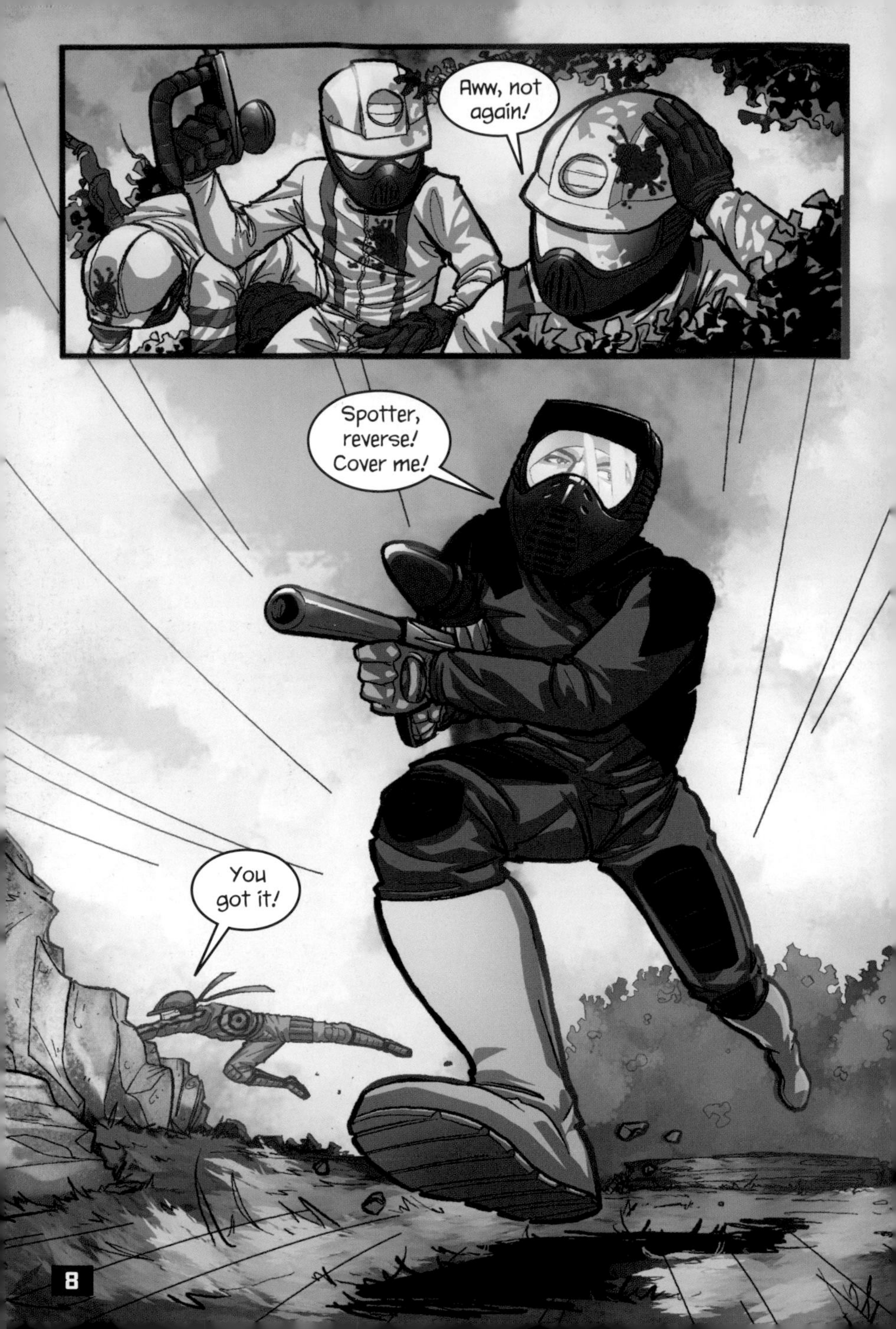
Aww, not again!
Spotter, reverse! Cover me!
You got it!

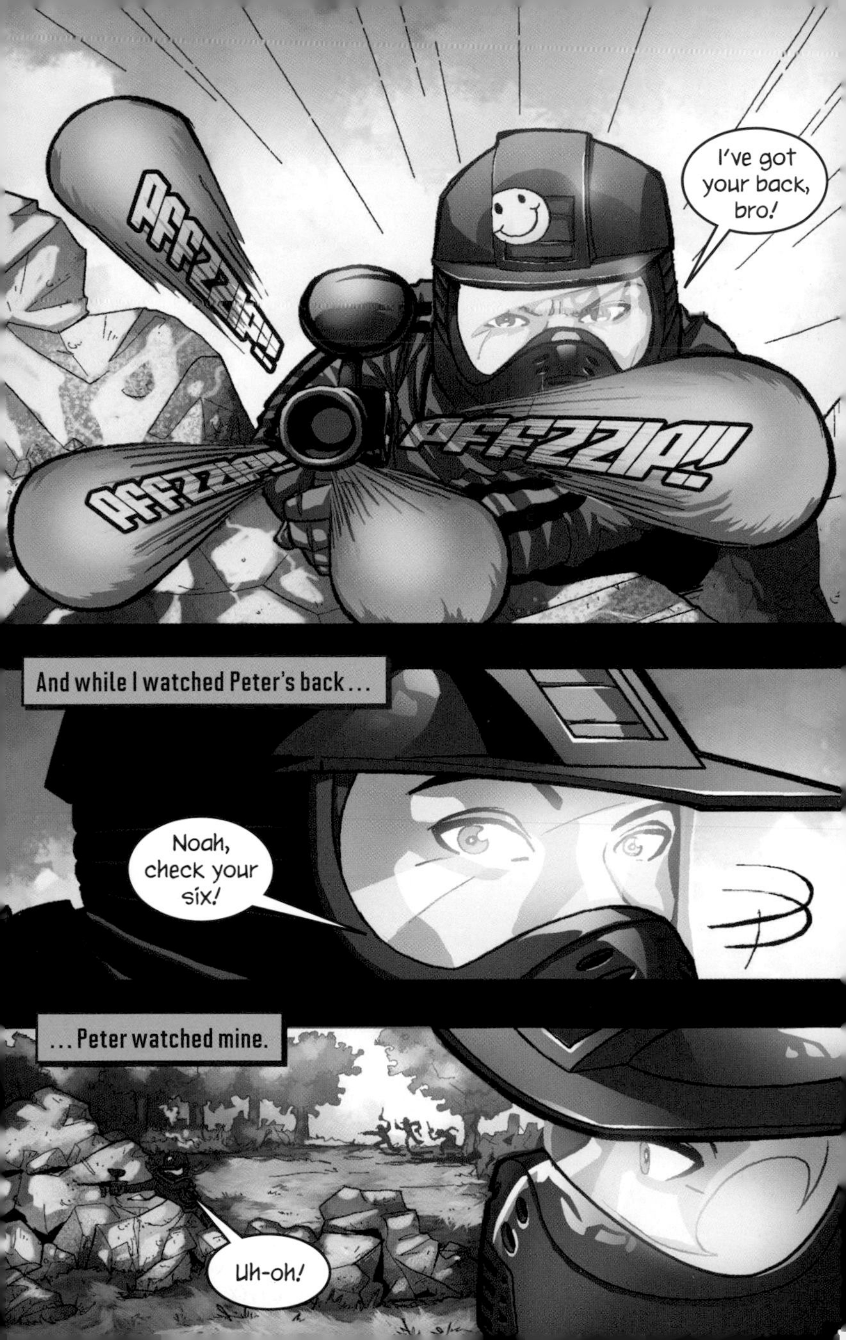
PFFZZIP!!
I've got your back, bro!
PFFZZIP!!
PFFZZIP!!
And while I watched Peter's back . . .
Noah, check your six!
. . . Peter watched mine.
Uh-oh!

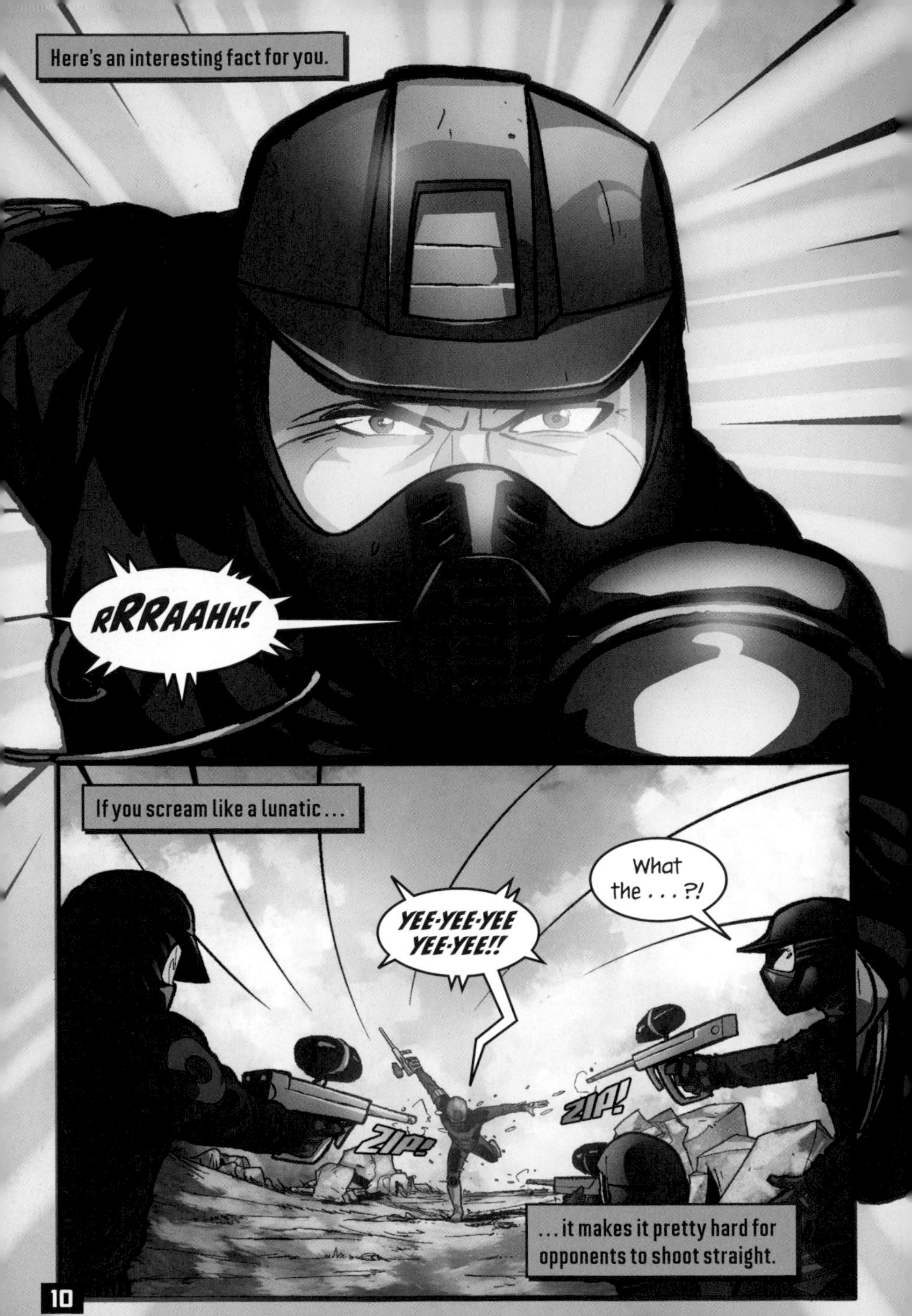
Here's an interesting fact for you.
RRRAAHH!
If you scream like a lunatic . . .
YEE-YEE-YEE YEE-YEE!!
What the . . . ?!
ZIP!
ZIP!
. . . it makes it pretty hard for opponents to shoot straight.

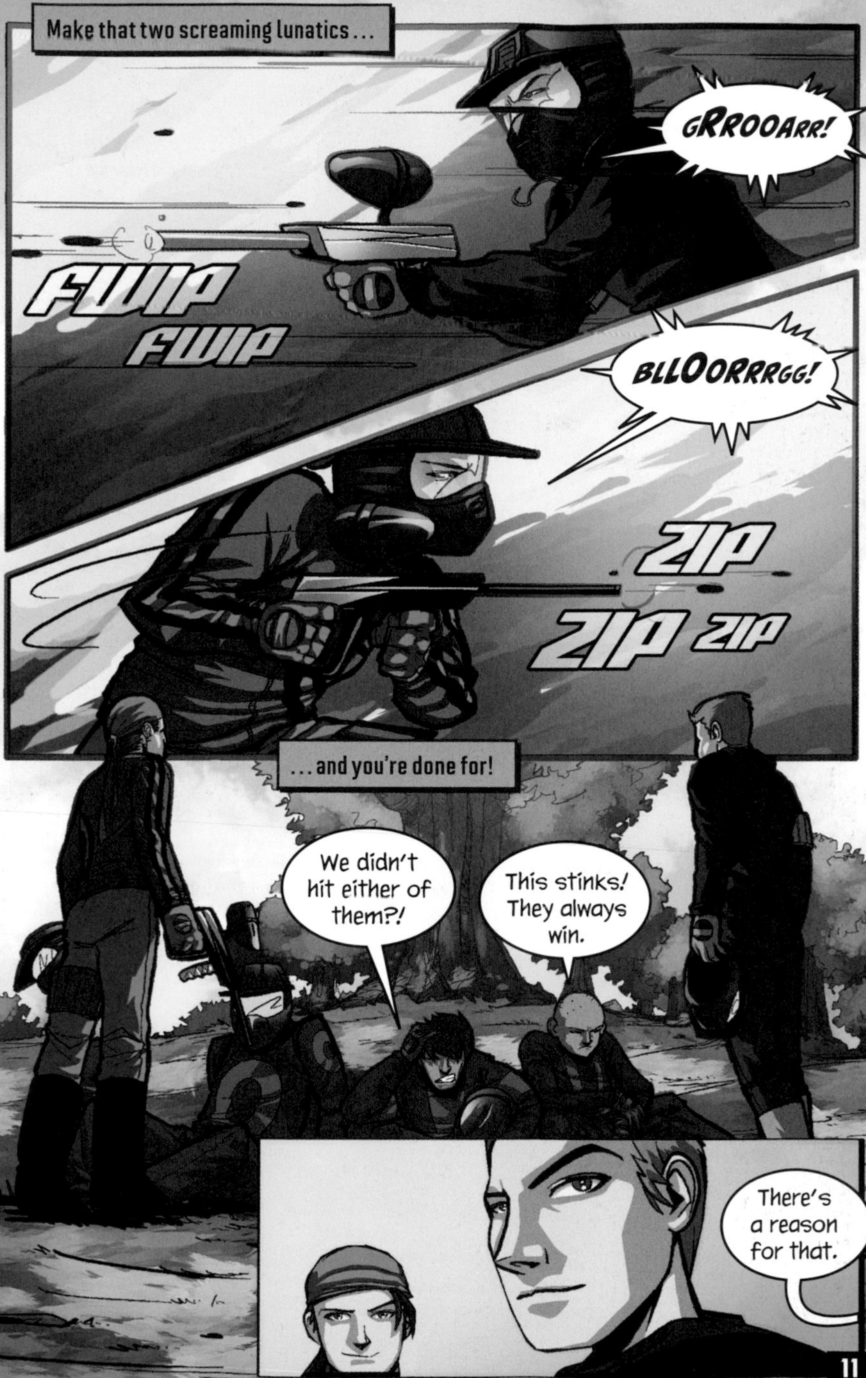

Make that two screaming lunatics . . .
GRROOARR!
FWIP
FWIP
BLLOORRRGG!
ZIP
ZIP ZIP
. . . and you're done for!
We didn't hit either of them?!
This stinks! They always win.
There's a reason for that.

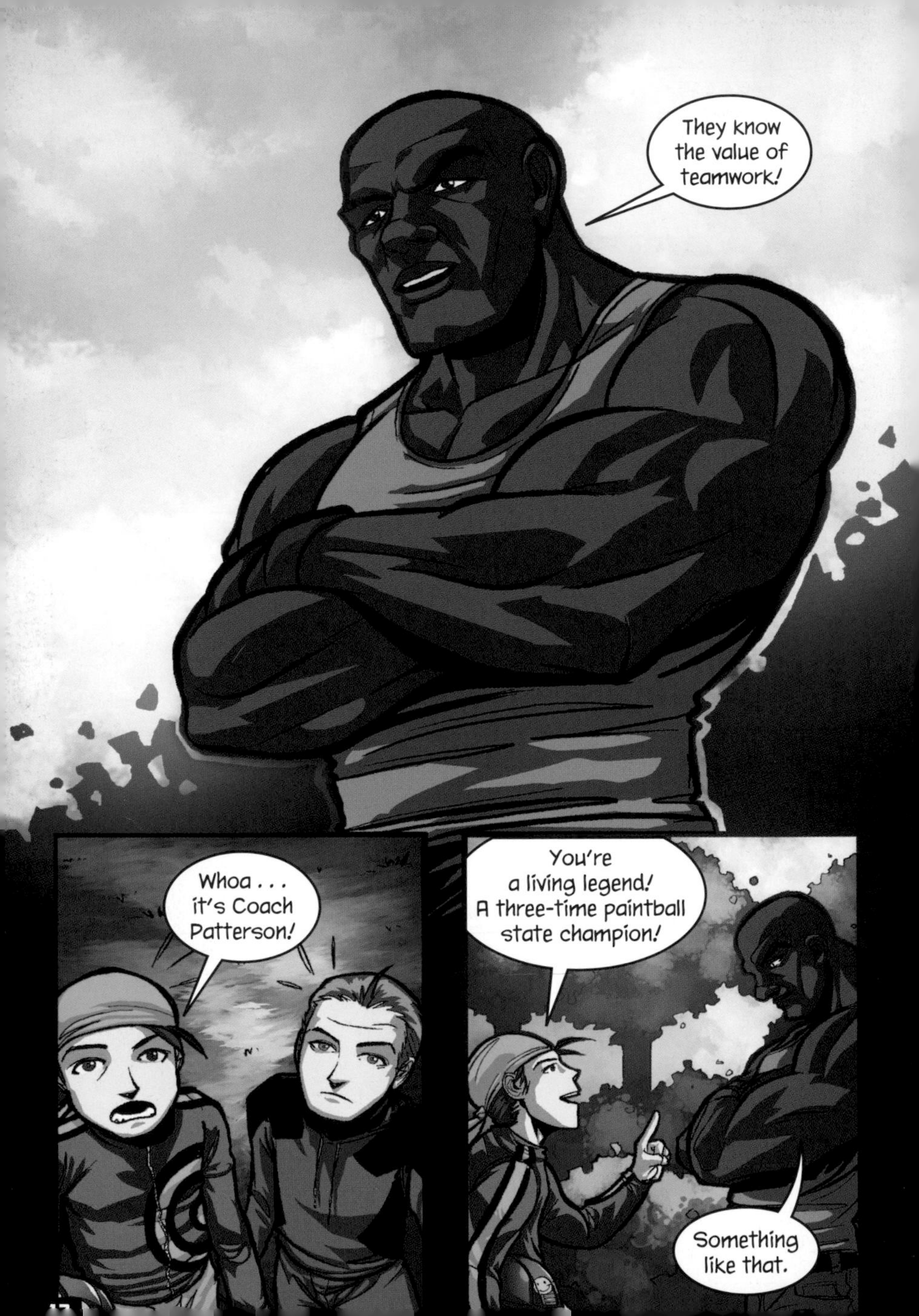
They know the value of teamwork!
Whoa . . . it's Coach Patterson!
You're a living legend! A three-time paintball state champion!
Something like that.

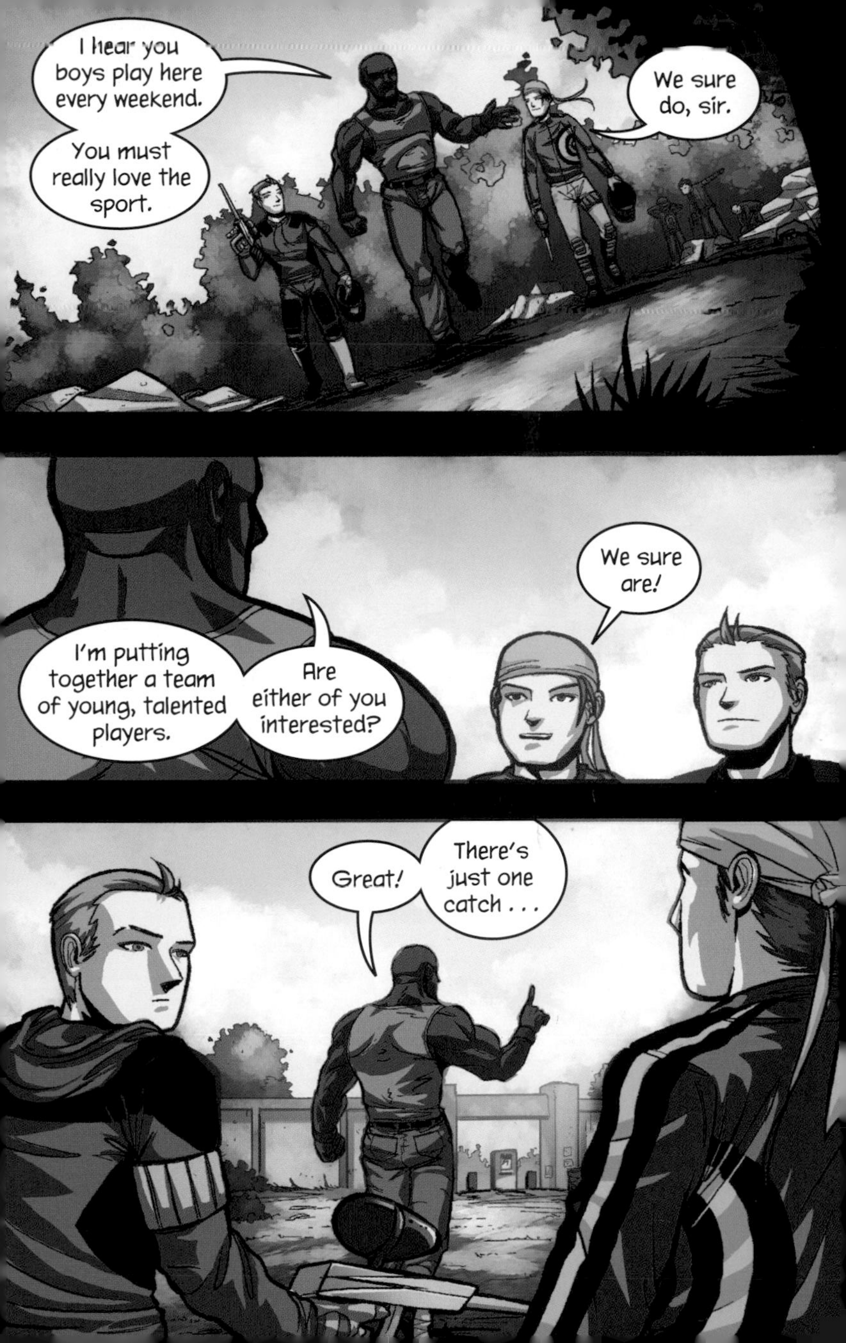
I hear you boys play here every weekend.
You must really love the sport.
We sure do, sir.
I'm putting together a team of young, talented players.
Are either of you interested?
We sure are!
Great!
There's just one catch . . .

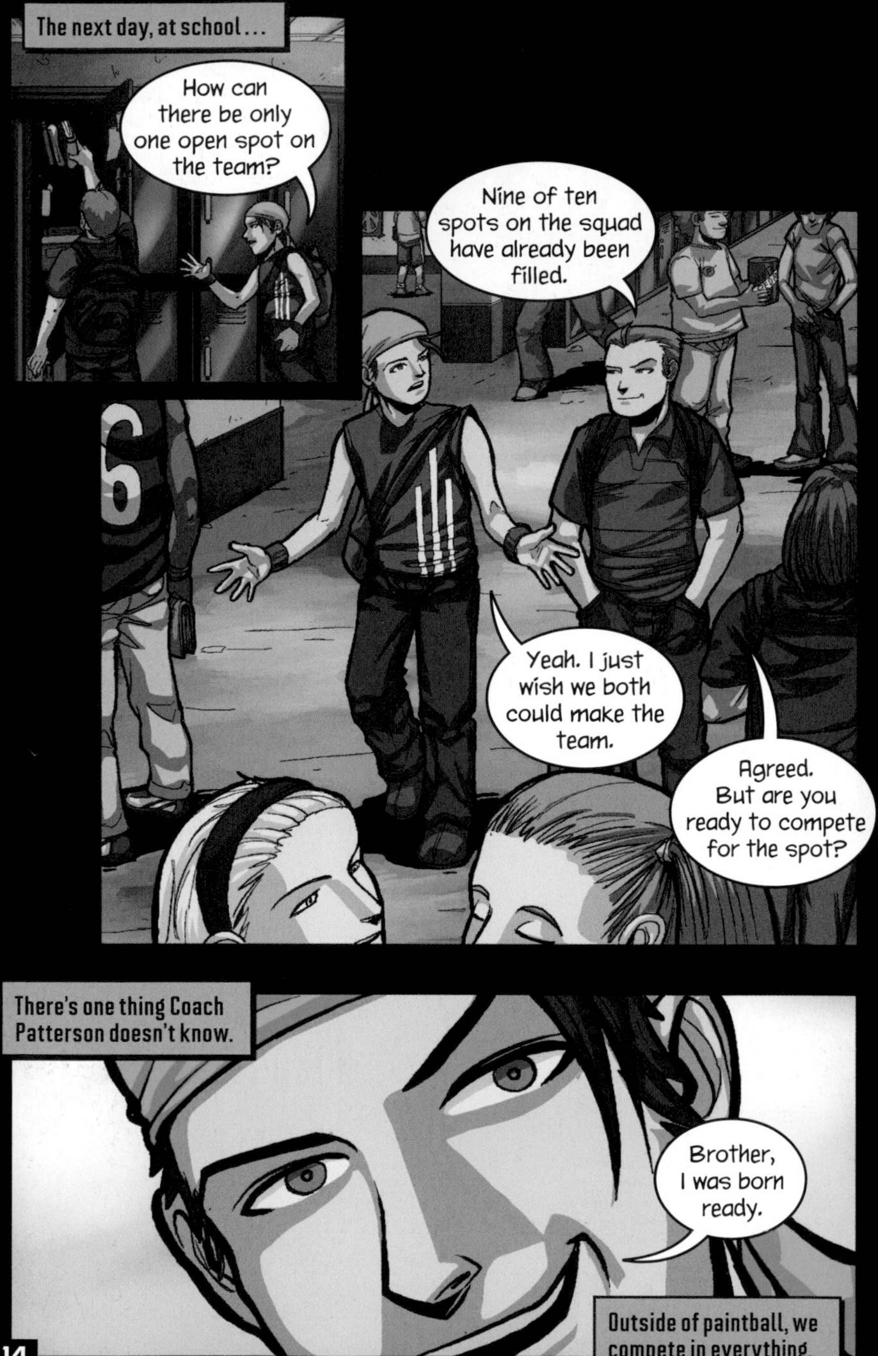
The next day, at school . . .
How can there be only one open spot on the team?
Nine of ten spots on the squad have already been filled.
Yeah. I just wish we both could make the team.
Agreed. But are you ready to compete for the spot?
There's one thing Coach Patterson doesn't know.
Brother, I was born ready.
Outside of paintball, we compete in everything.

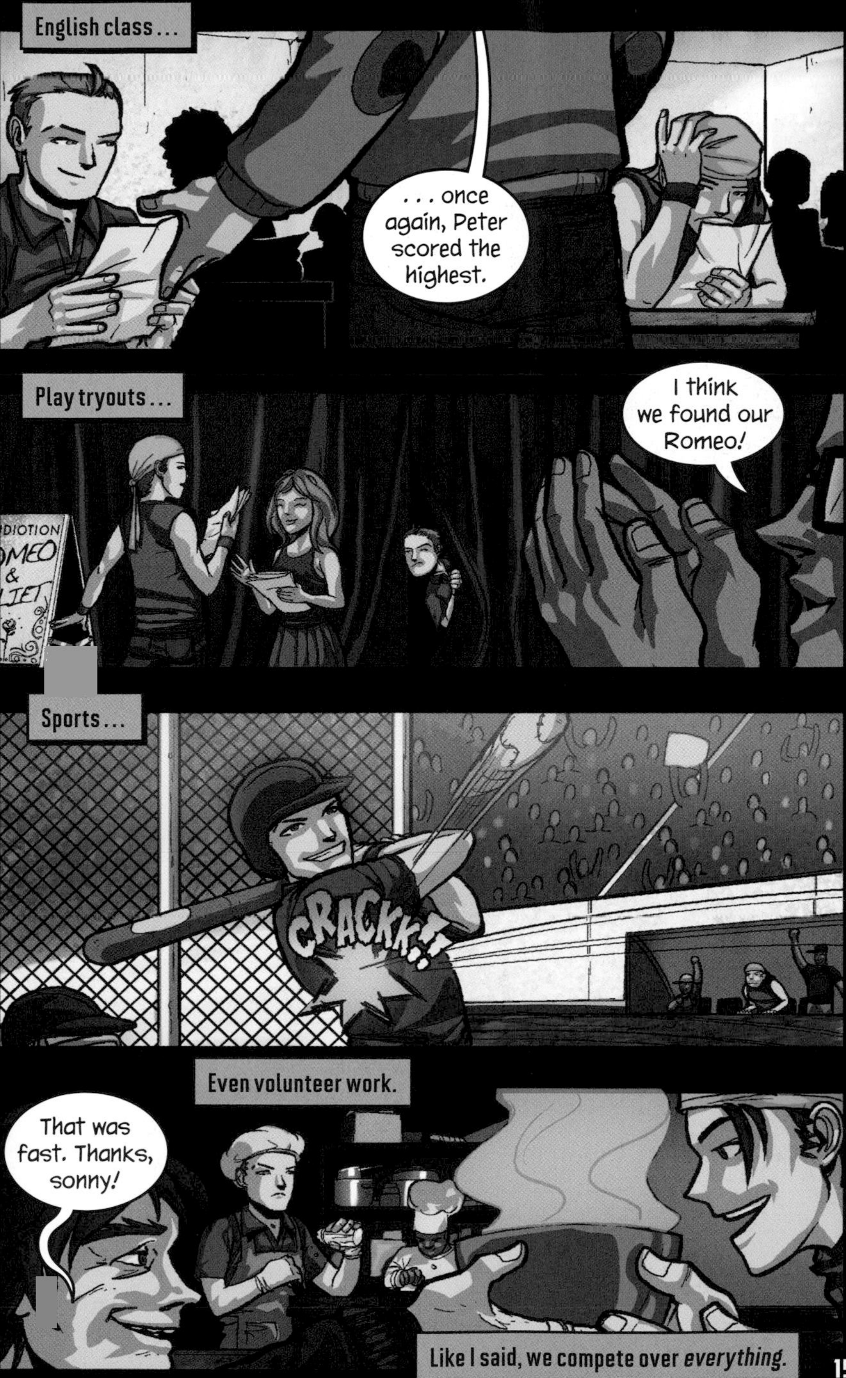
English class . . .
. . . once again, Peter scored the highest.
Play tryouts . . .
I think we found our Romeo!
Sports . . .
CRACKK!!
Even volunteer work.
That was fast. Thanks, sonny!
Like I said, we compete over *everything*.

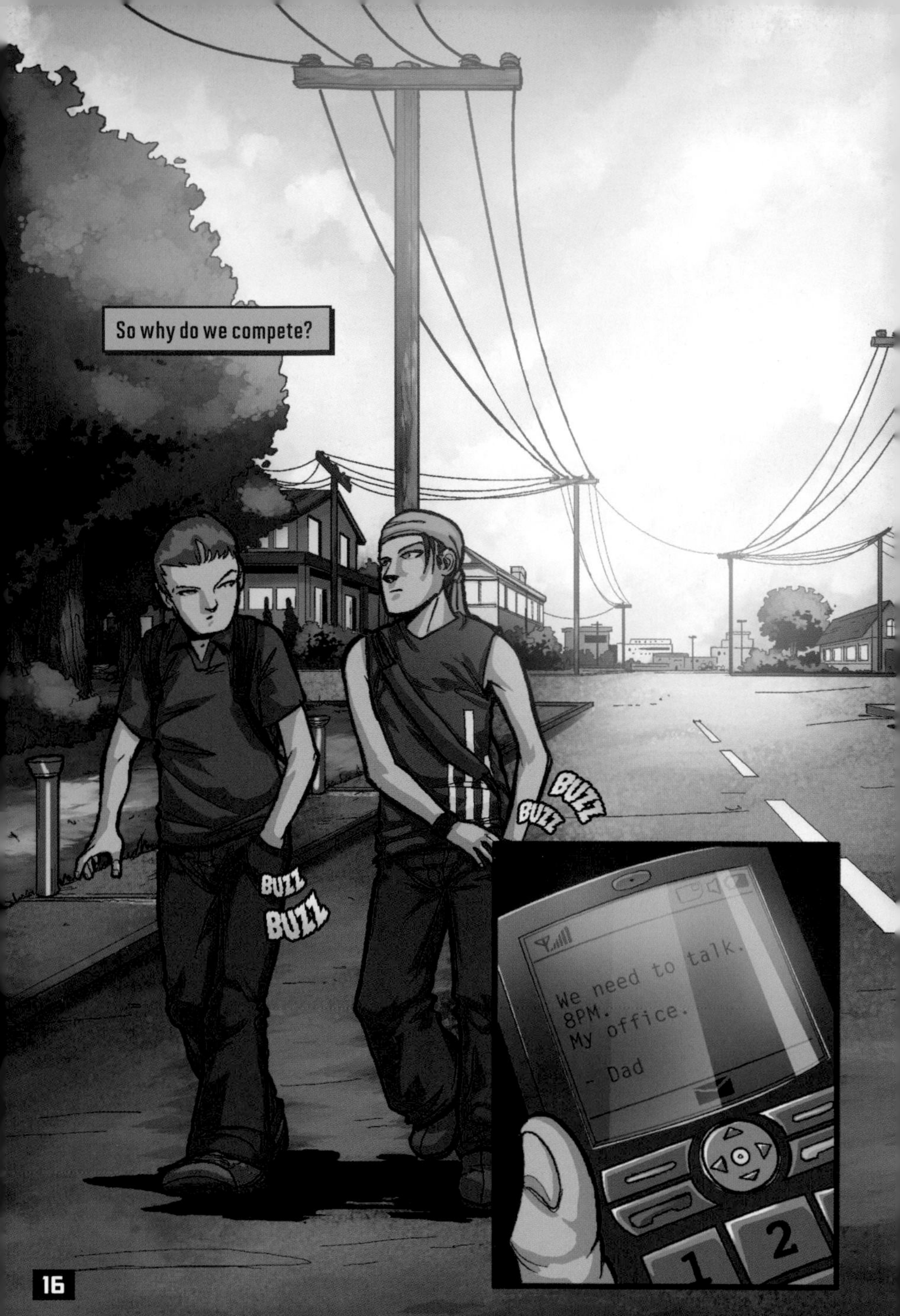

So why do we compete?
BUZZ
BUZZ
BUZZ
BUZZ
We need to talk.
8PM.
My office.
- Dad

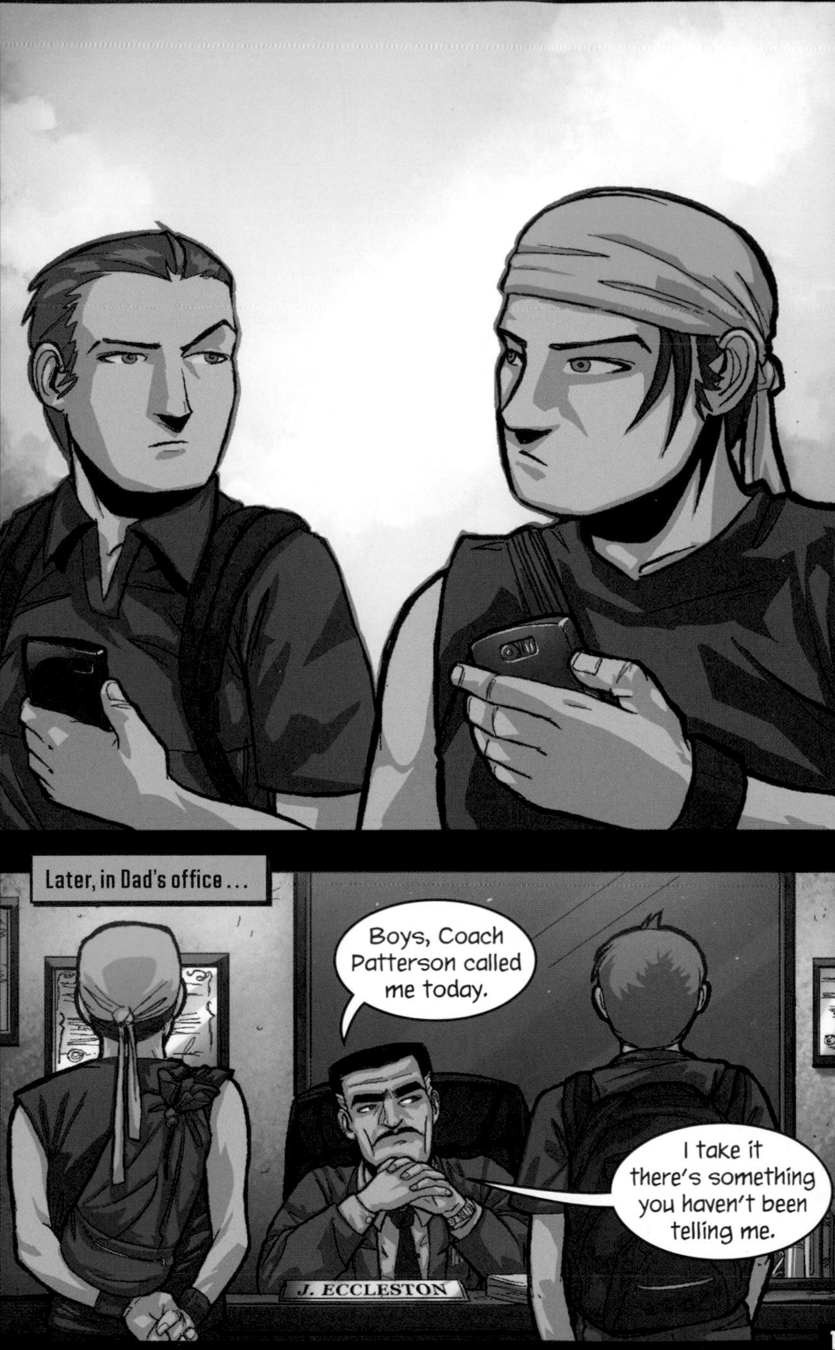
Later, in Dad's office . . .
Boys, Coach Patterson called me today.
I take it there's something you haven't been telling me.
J. ECCLESTON

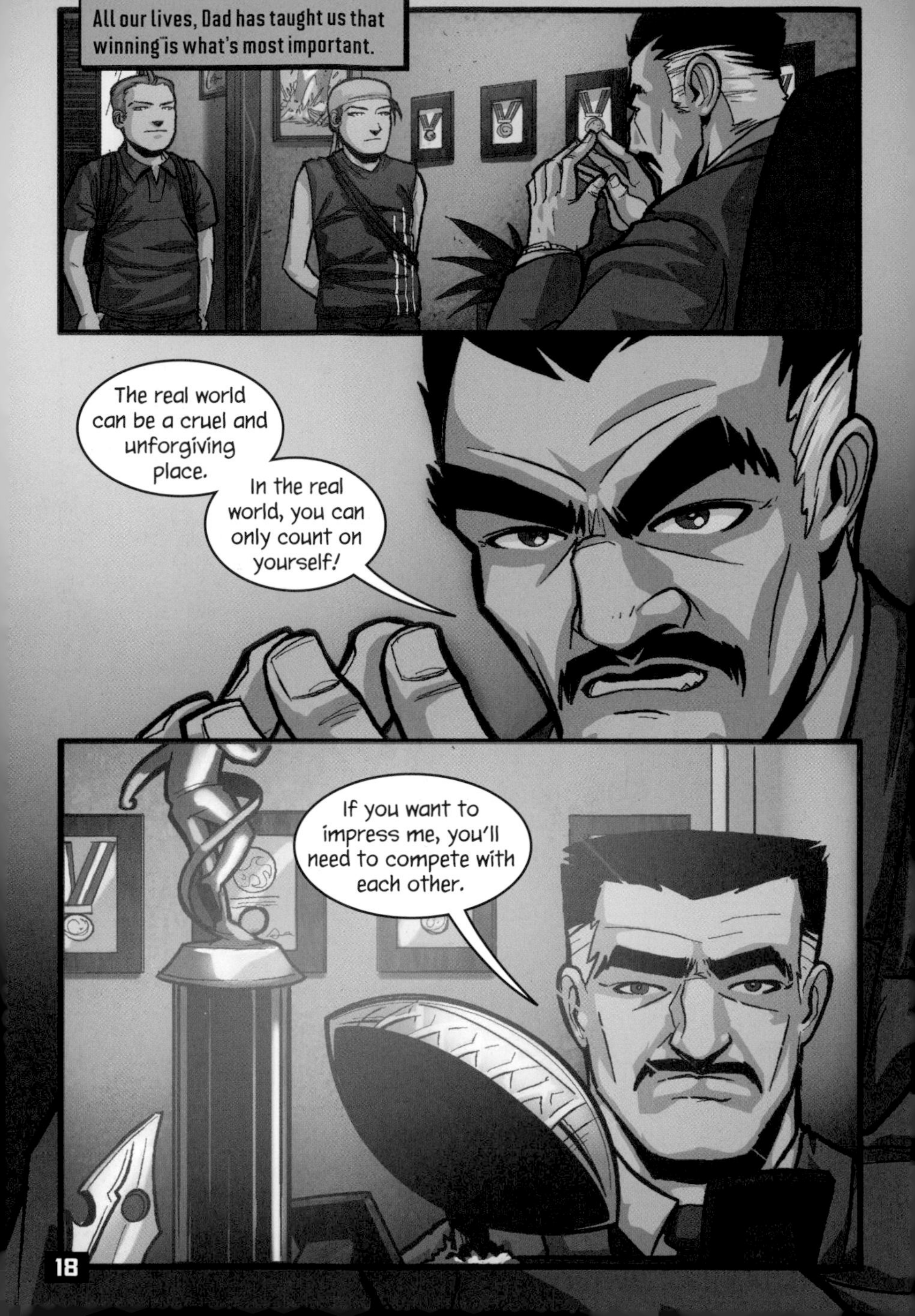
All our lives, Dad has taught us that winning is what's most important.
The real world can be a cruel and unforgiving place.
In the real world, you can only count on yourself!
If you want to impress me, you'll need to compete with each other.

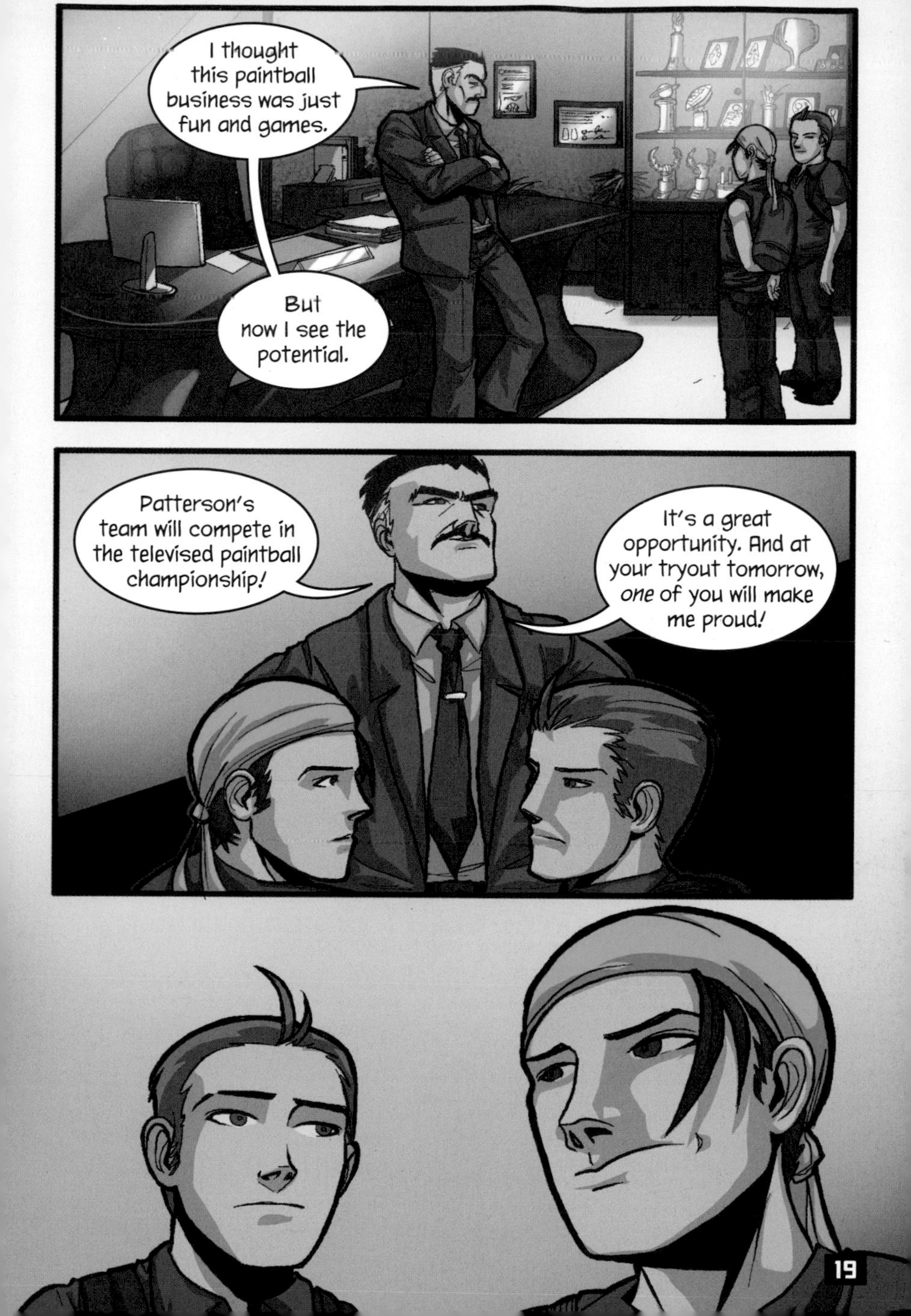

I thought this paintball business was just fun and games.
But now I see the potential.
Patterson's team will compete in the televised paintball championship!
It's a great opportunity. And at your tryout tomorrow, *one* of you will make me proud!

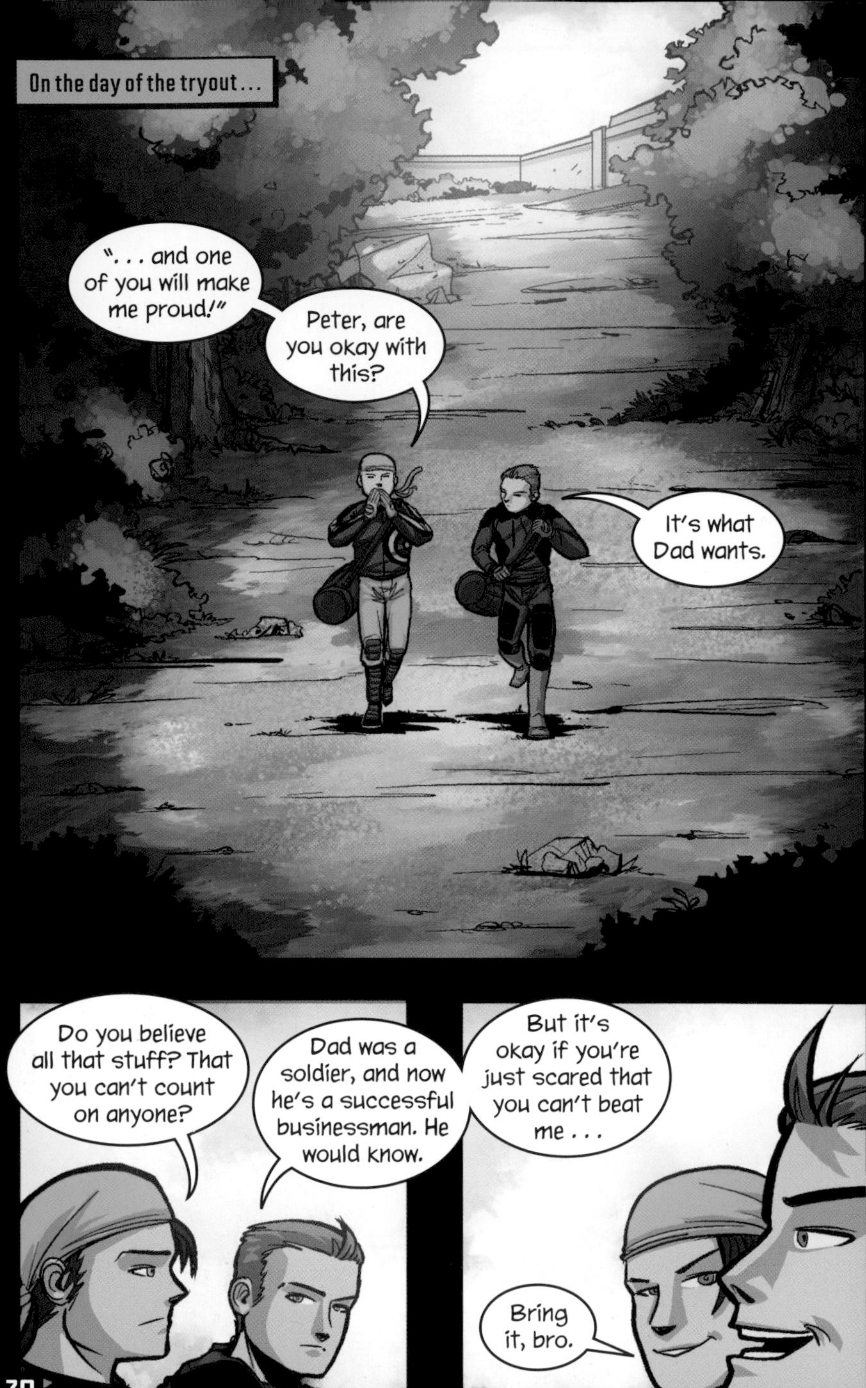
On the day of the tryout . . .
". . . and one of you will make me proud!"
Peter, are you okay with this?
It's what Dad wants.
Do you believe all that stuff? That you can't count on anyone?
Dad was a soldier, and now he's a successful businessman. He would know.
But it's okay if you're just scared that you can't beat me . . .
Bring it, bro.

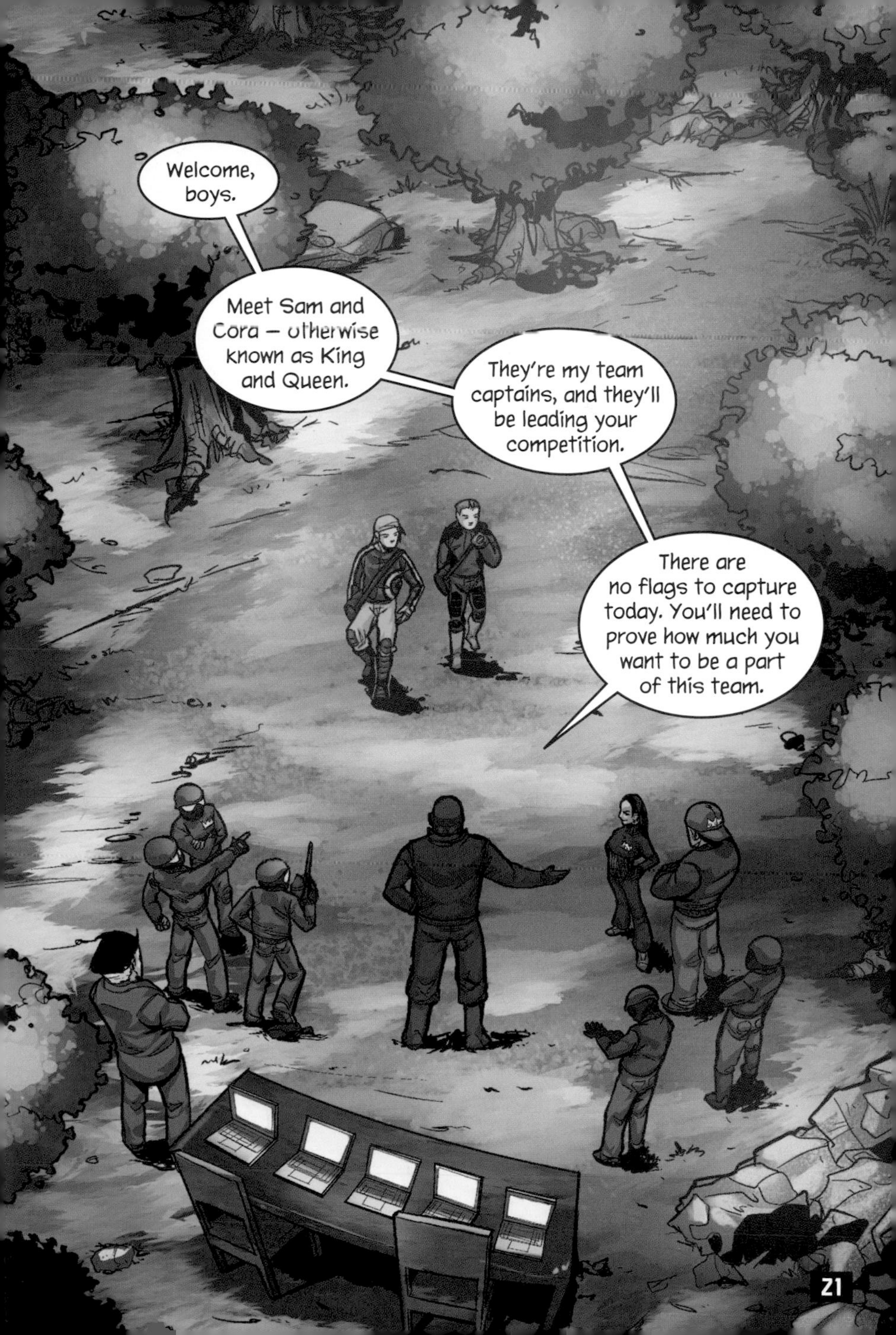
Welcome, boys.
Meet Sam and Cora — otherwise known as King and Queen.
They're my team captains, and they'll be leading your competition.
There are no flags to capture today. You'll need to prove how much you want to be a part of this team.

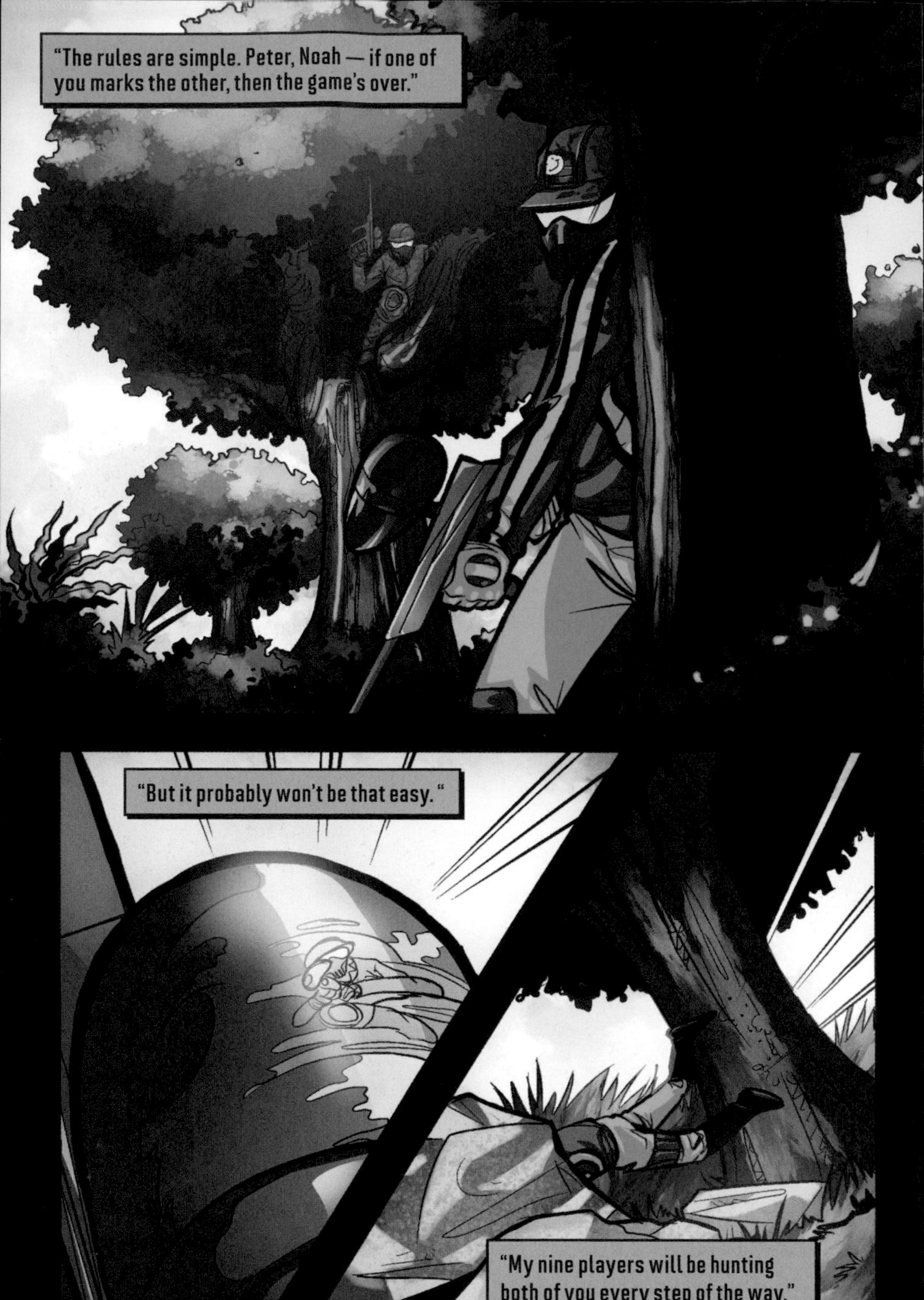
"The rules are simple. Peter, Noah — if one of you marks the other, then the game's over."
"But it probably won't be that easy. "
"My nine players will be hunting both of you every step of the way."

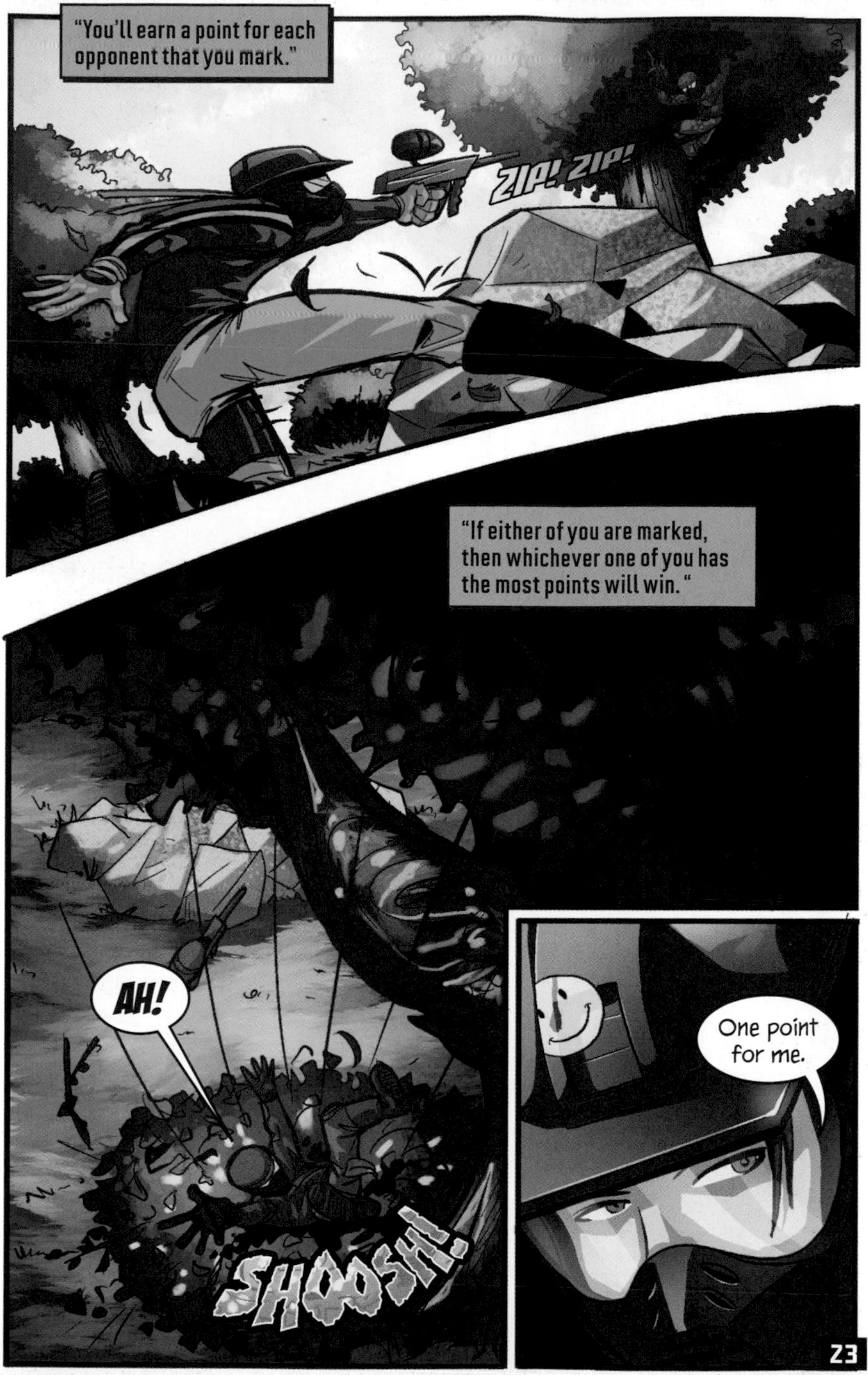
"You'll earn a point for each opponent that you mark."
ZIP! ZIP!
"If either of you are marked, then whichever one of you has the most points will win."
AH!
SHOOSH!
One point for me.

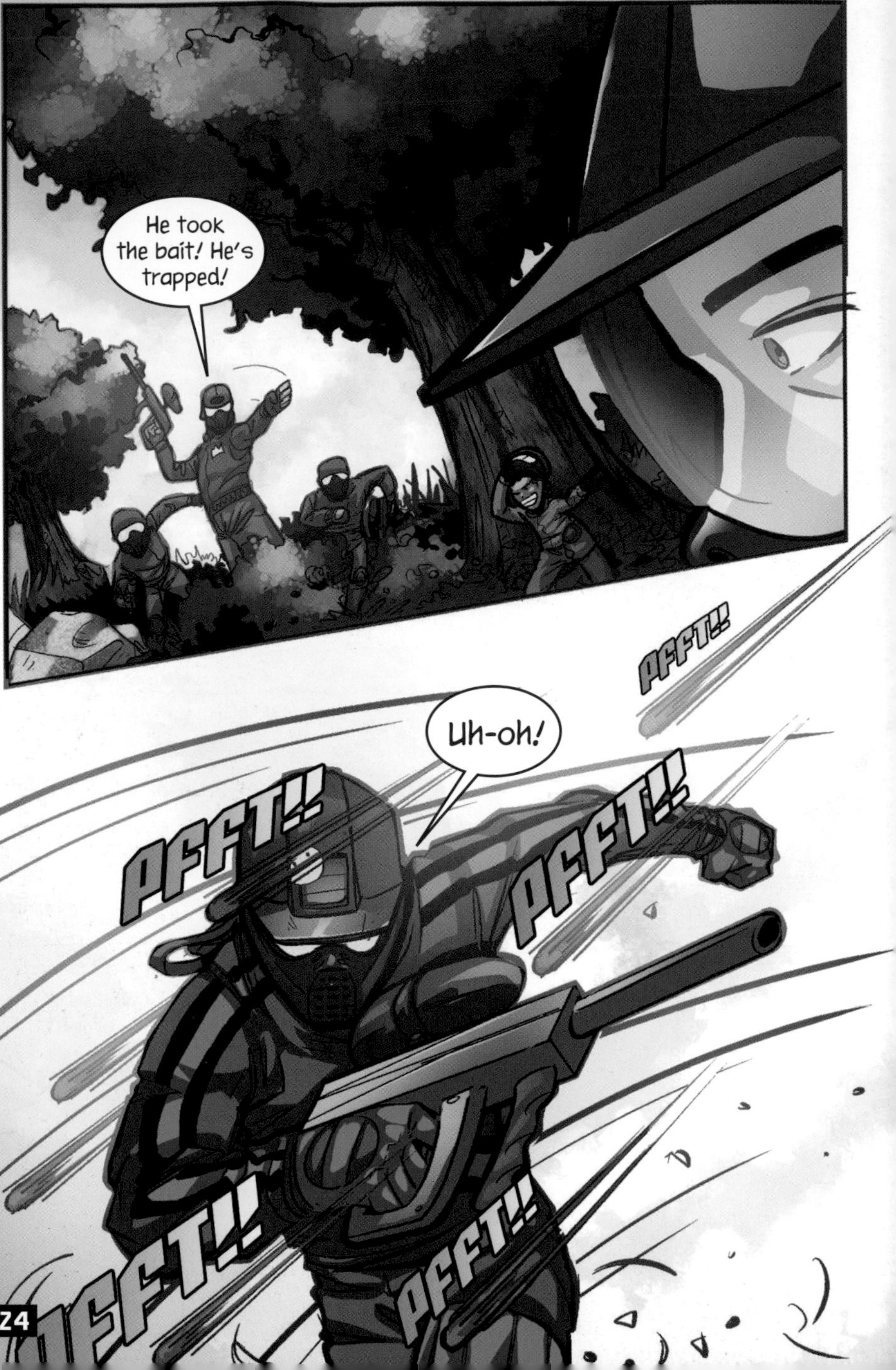
He took the bait! He's trapped!
PFFT!!
Uh-oh!
PFFT!!
PFFT!!
FFT!!
PFFT!!

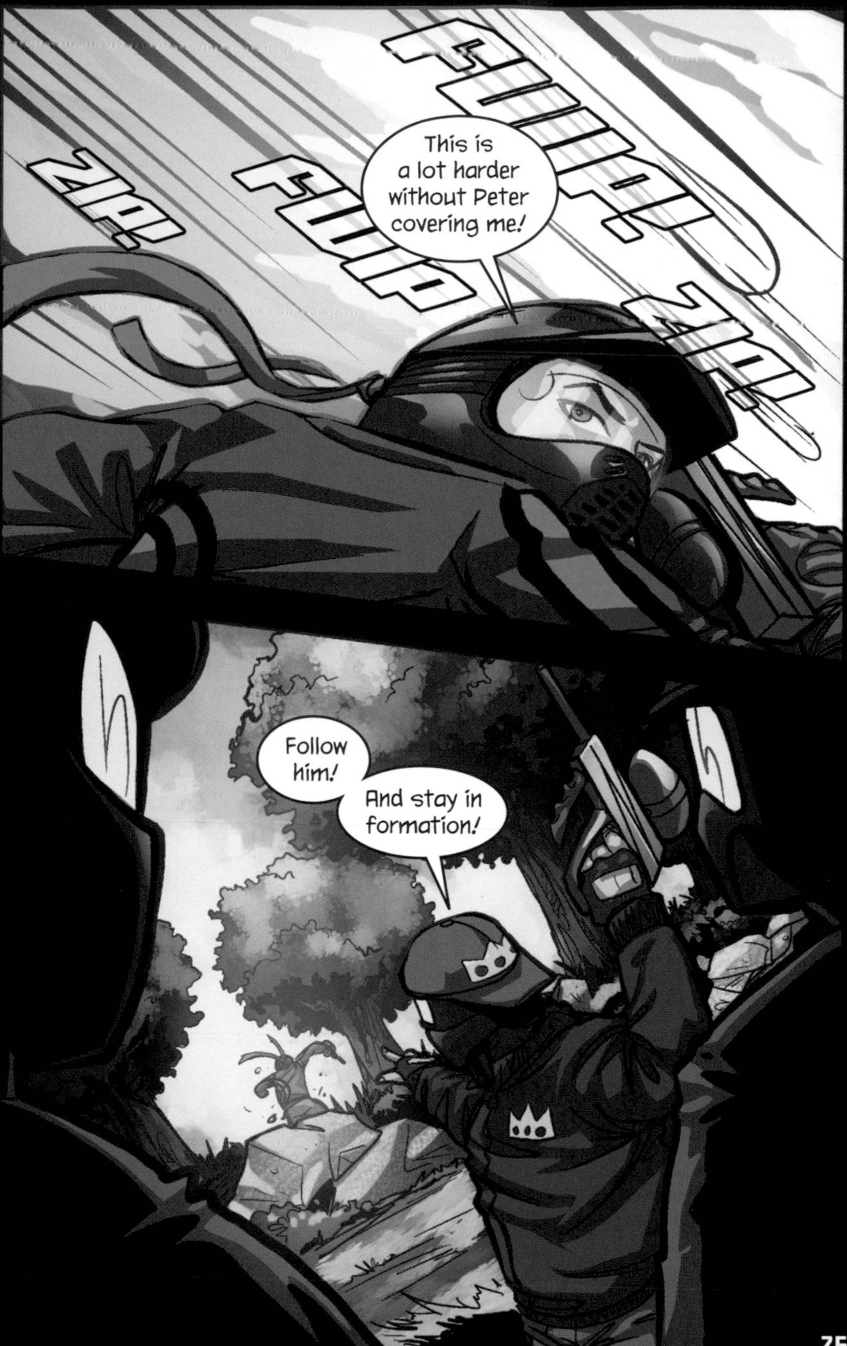
ZIP!
FWIP
FWIP!
ZIP! ZIP!
This is a lot harder without Peter covering me!
Follow him!
And stay in formation!

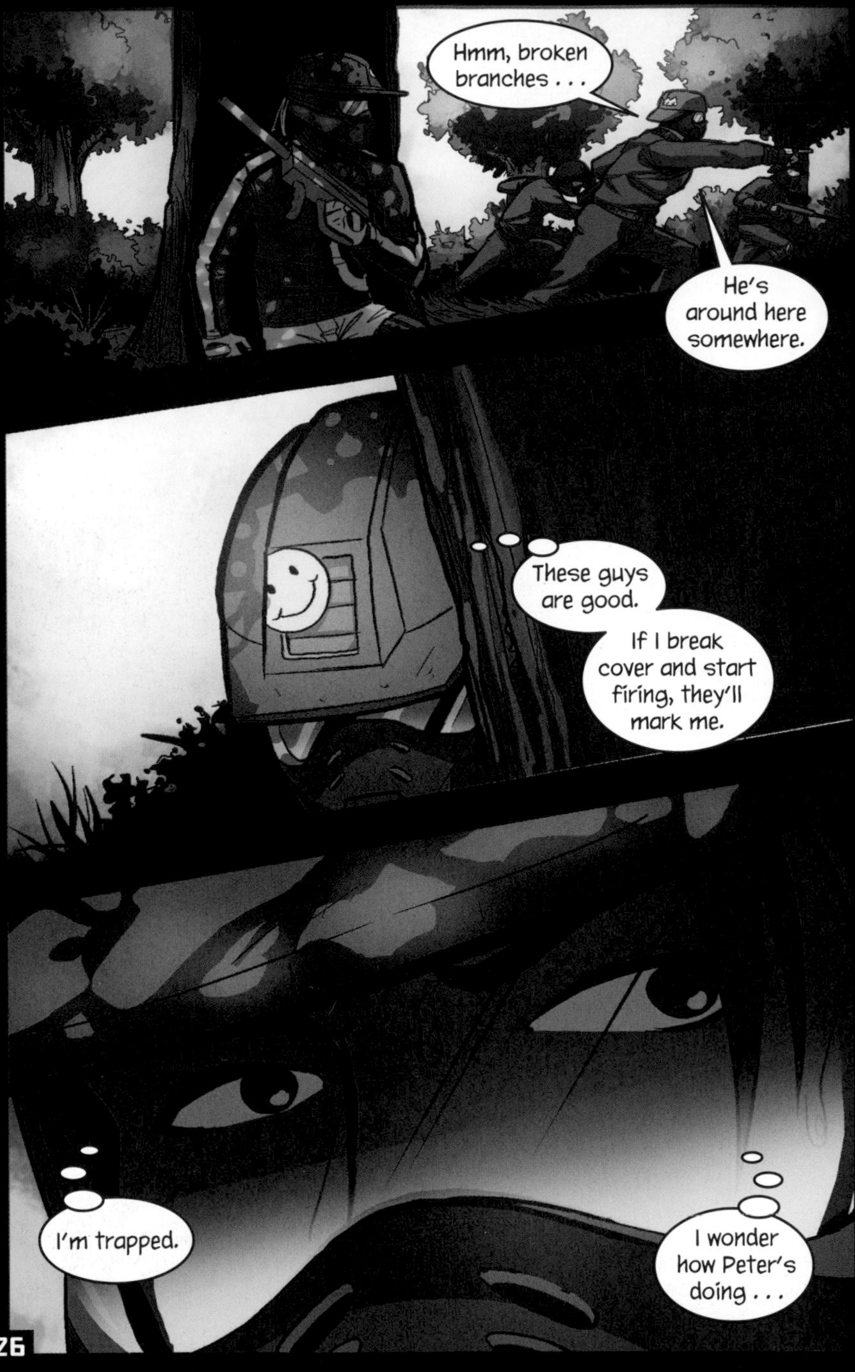
Hmm, broken branches . . .
He's around here somewhere.
These guys are good.
If I break cover and start firing, they'll mark me.
I'm trapped.
I wonder how Peter's doing . . .

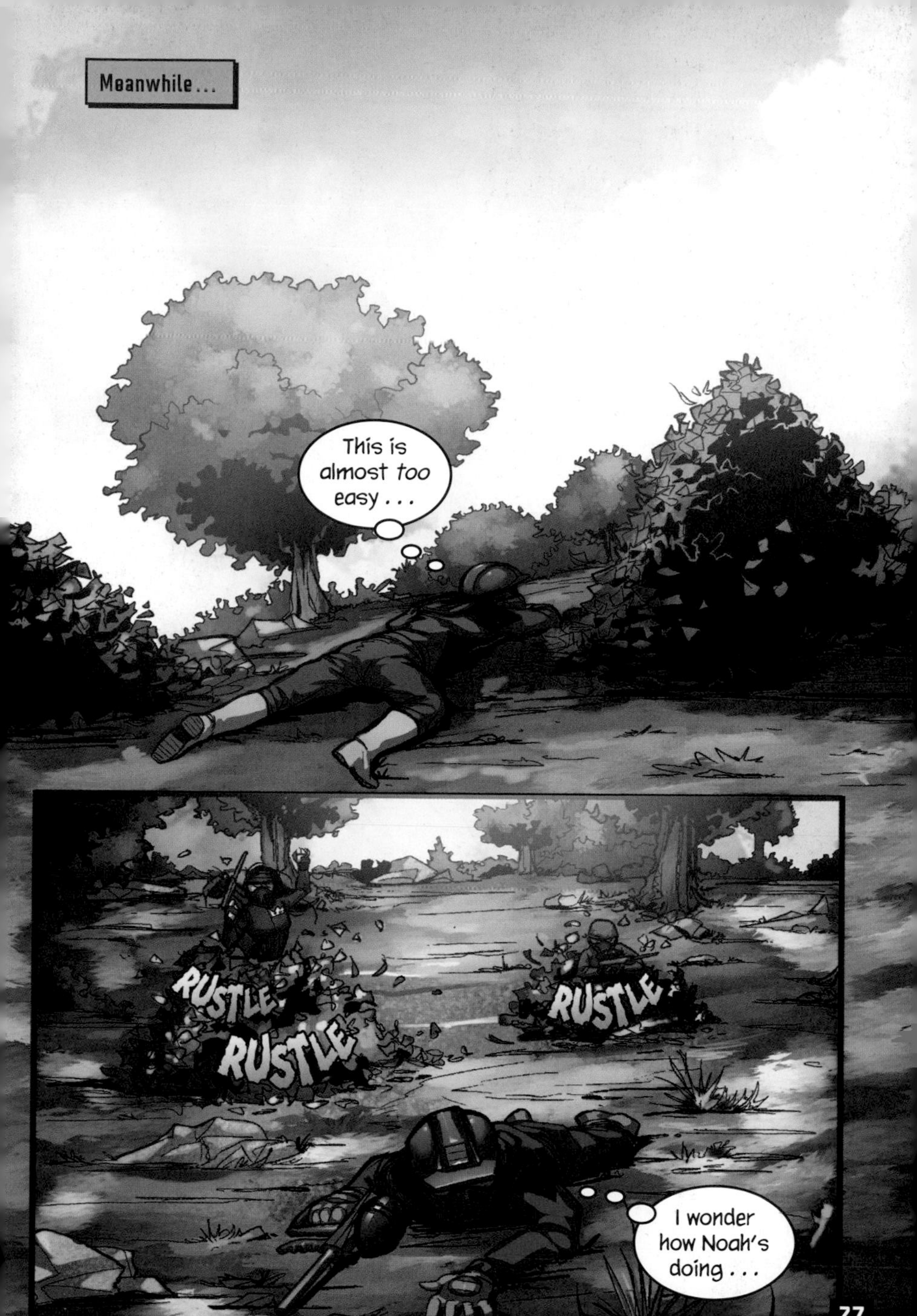
Meanwhile...
This is almost *too* easy . . .
RUSTLE
RUSTLE
RUSTLE
I wonder how Noah's doing . . .

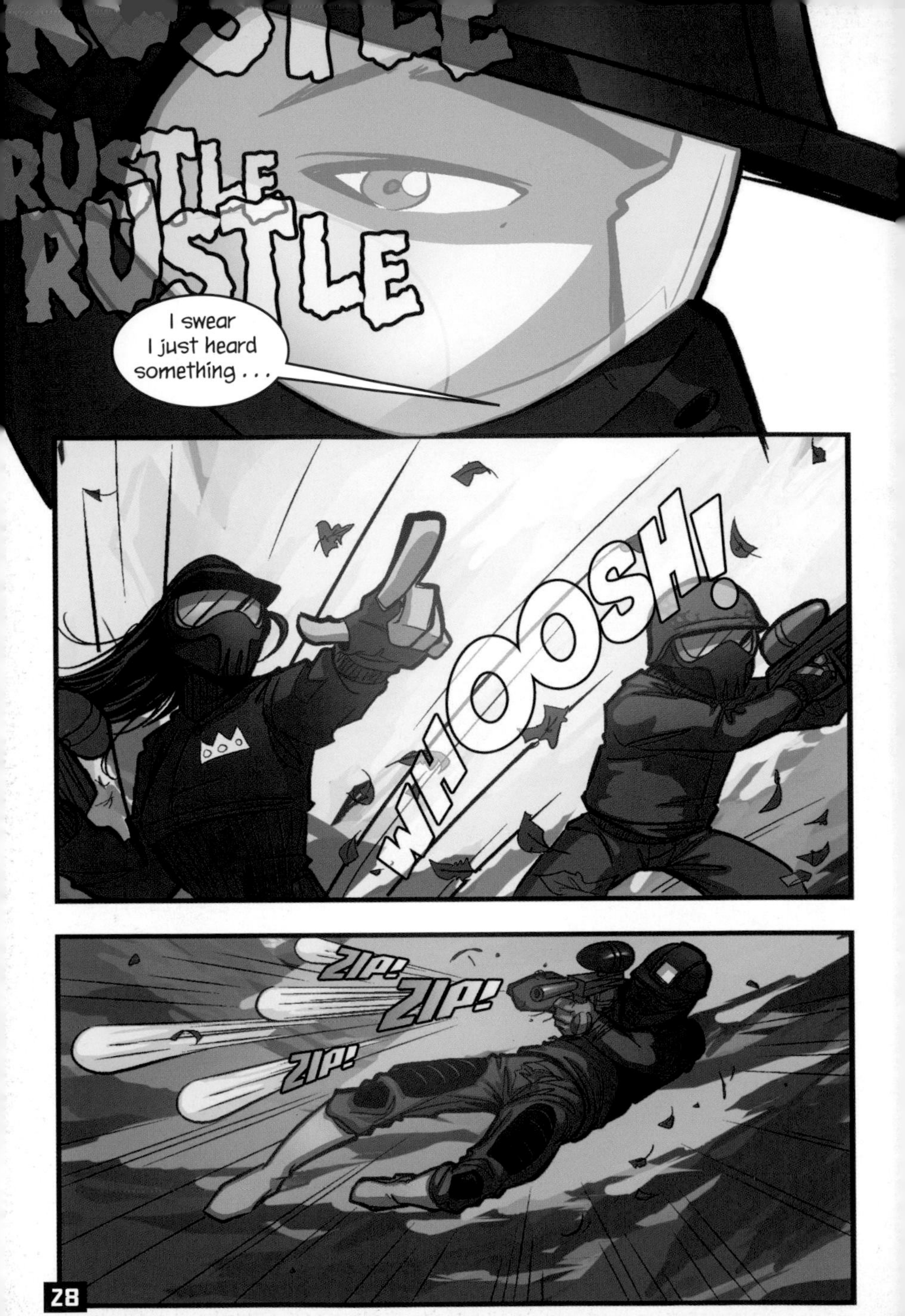
RUSTLE
RUSTLE
I swear I just heard something . . .
WHOOSH!
ZIP!
ZIP!
ZIP!

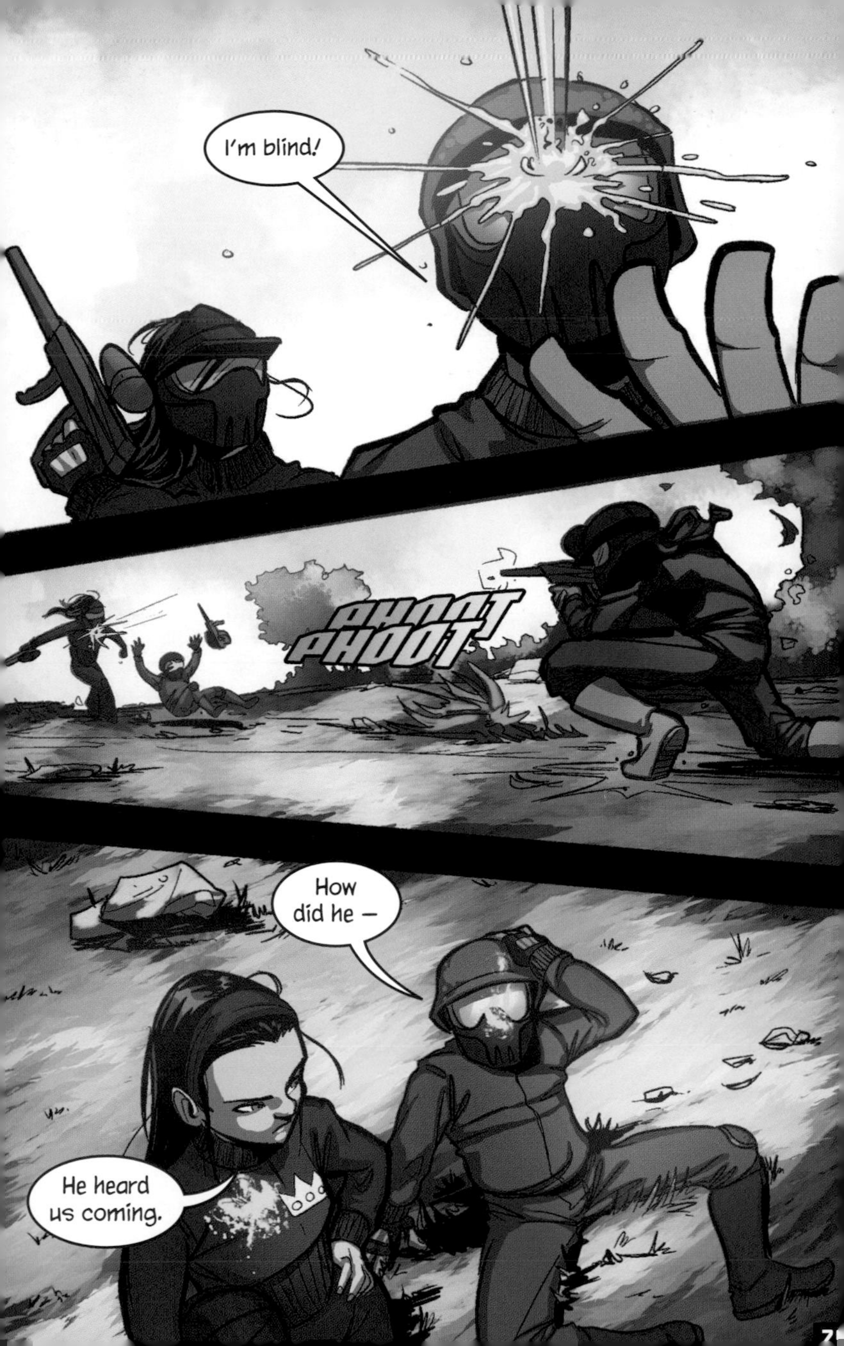
I'm blind!
PHOOT PHOOT
How did he —
He heard us coming.

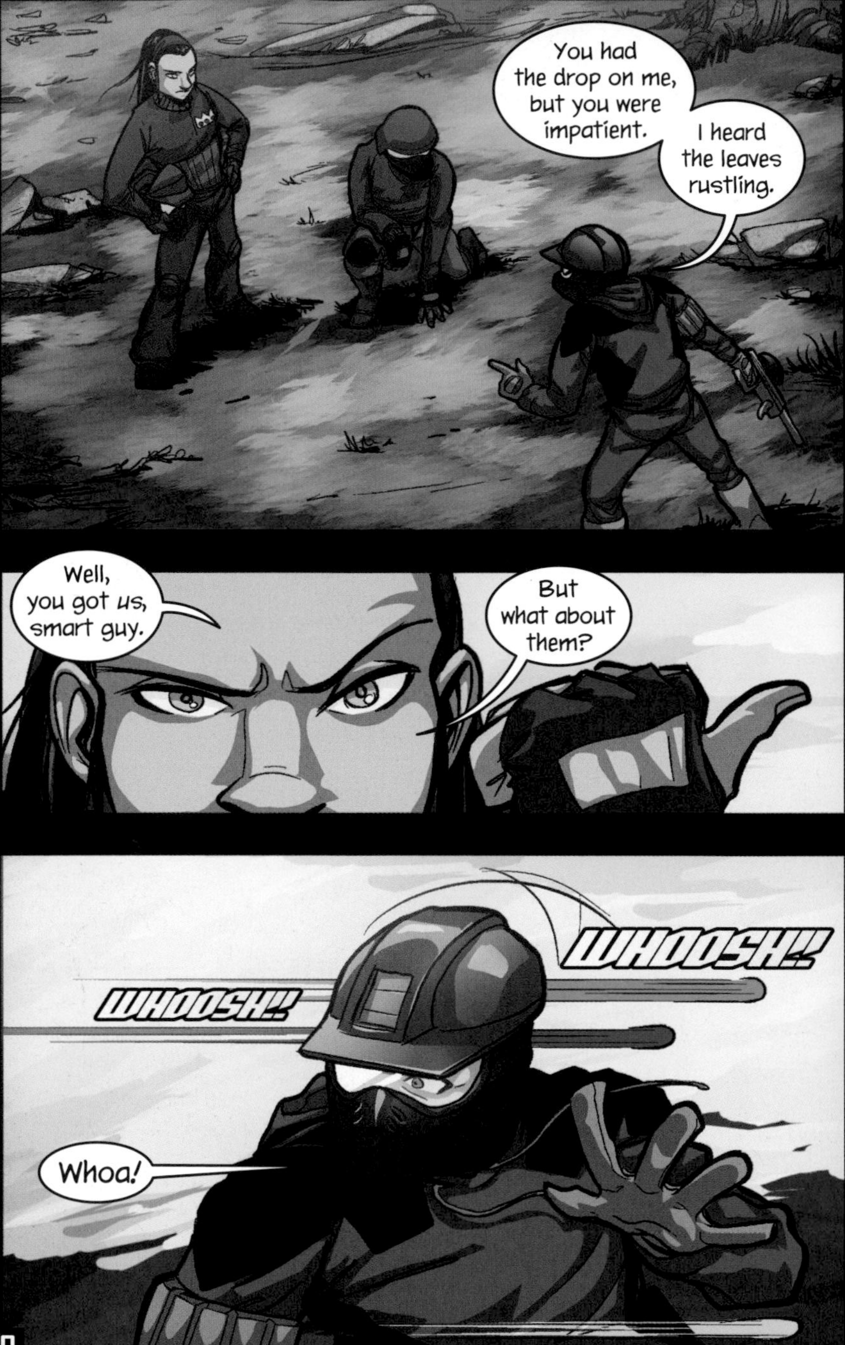
You had the drop on me, but you were impatient.
I heard the leaves rustling.
Well, you got us, smart guy.
But what about them?
WHOOSH!!
WHOOSH!!
Whoa!

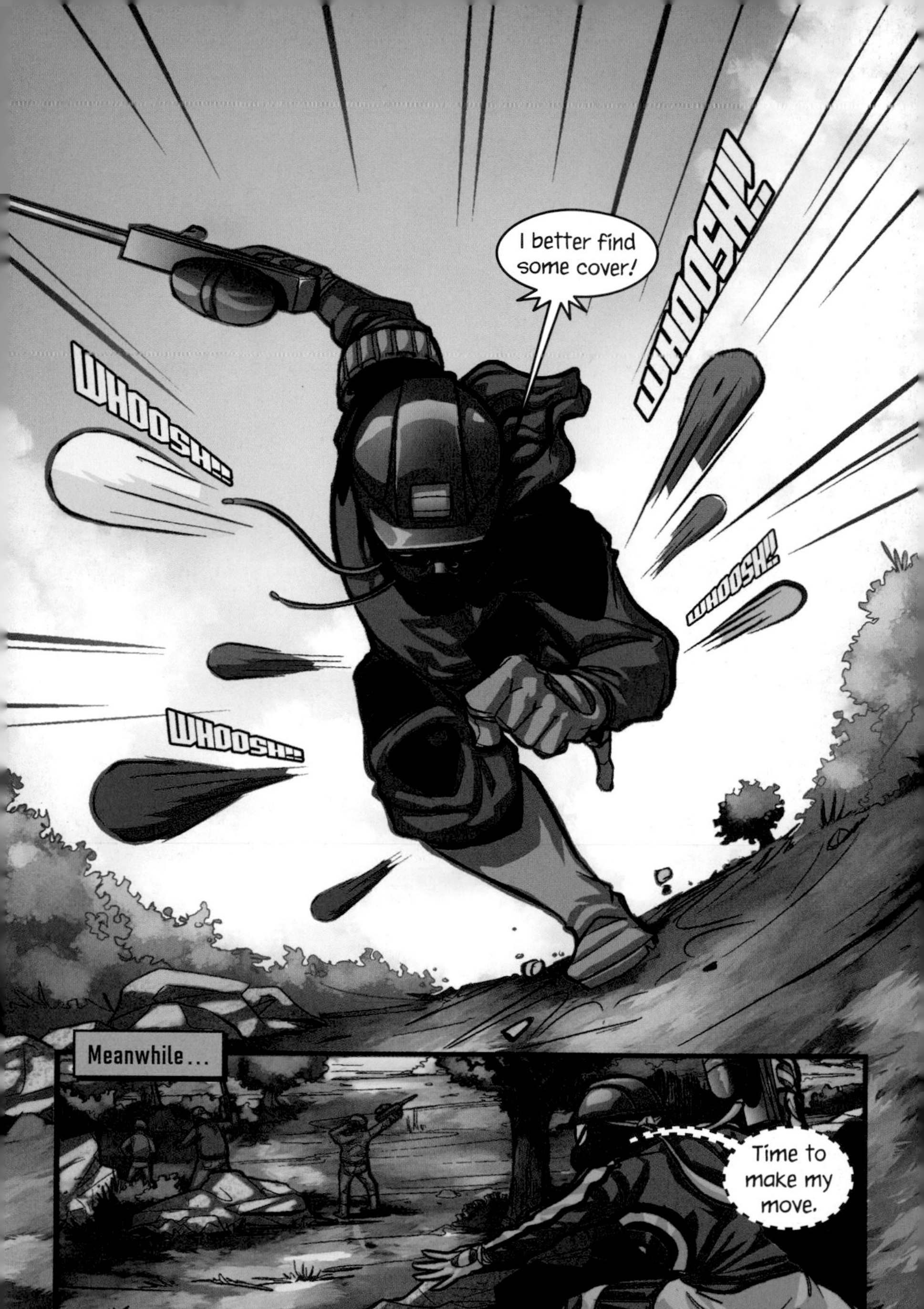

I better find some cover!
WHOOSH!!
WHOOSH!!
WHOOSH!!
WHOOSH!!
Meanwhile . . .
Time to make my move.

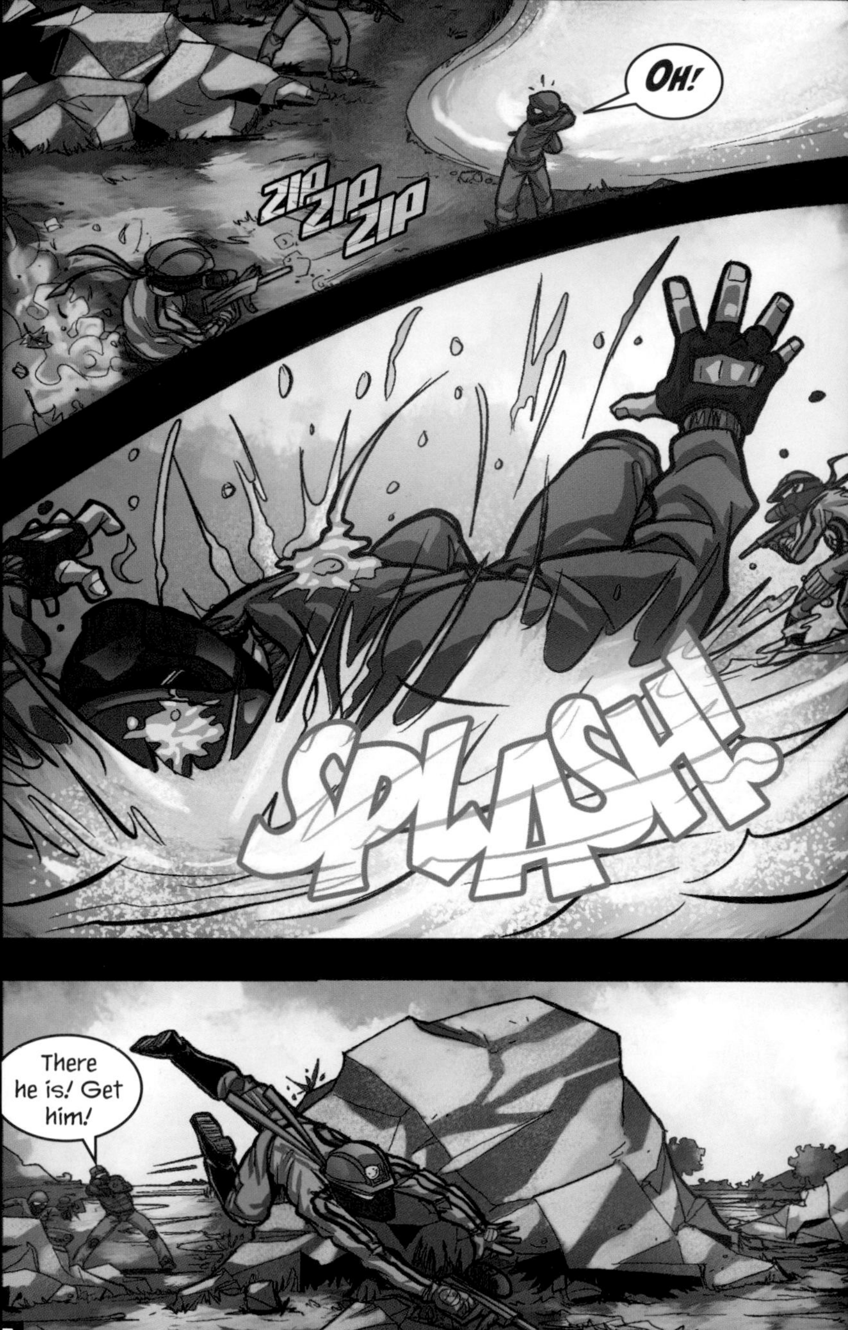
OH!
ZIP ZIP ZIP
SPLASH!
There he is! Get him!

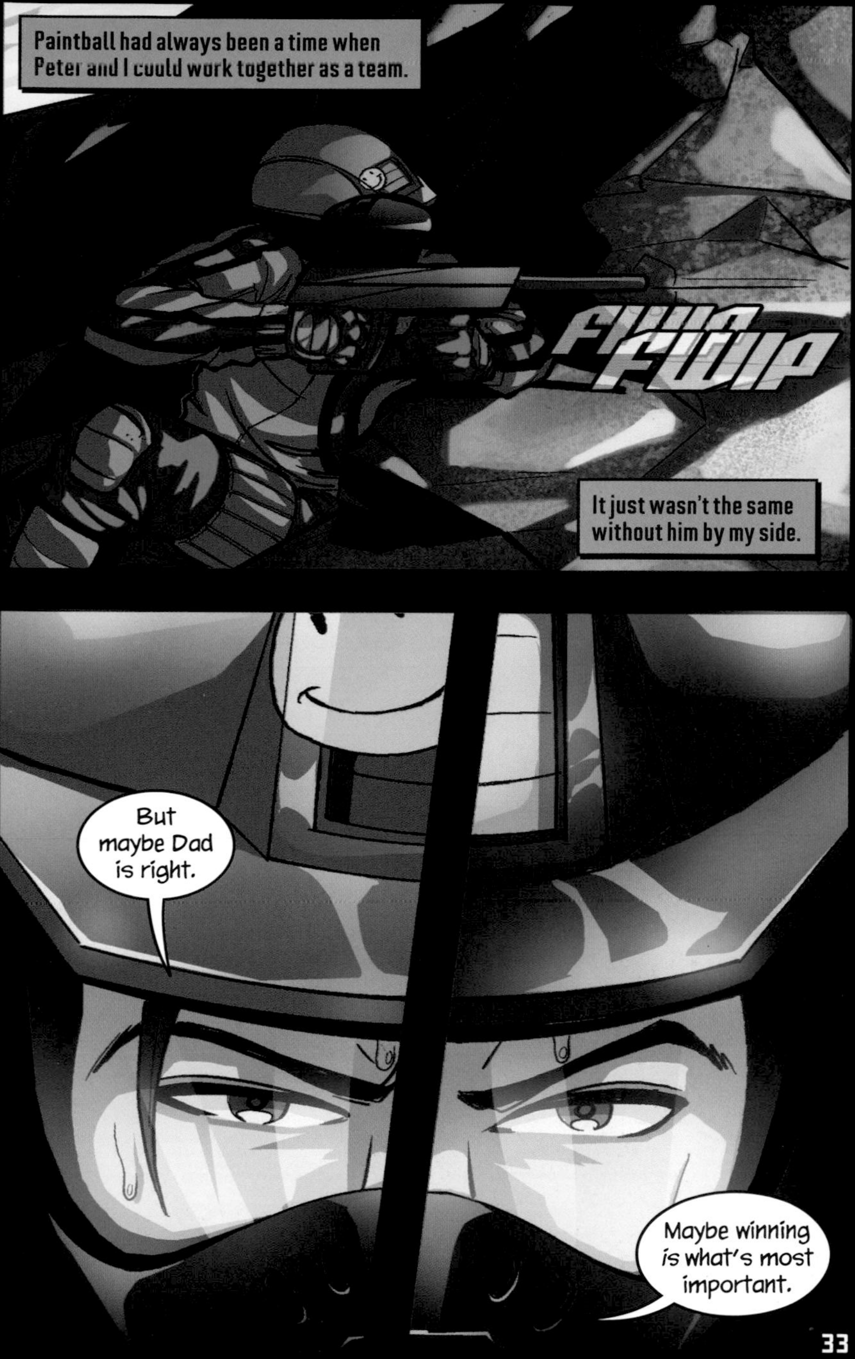
Paintball had always been a time when Peter and I could work together as a team.
FWIP
It just wasn't the same without him by my side.
But maybe Dad is right.
Maybe winning *is* what's most important.

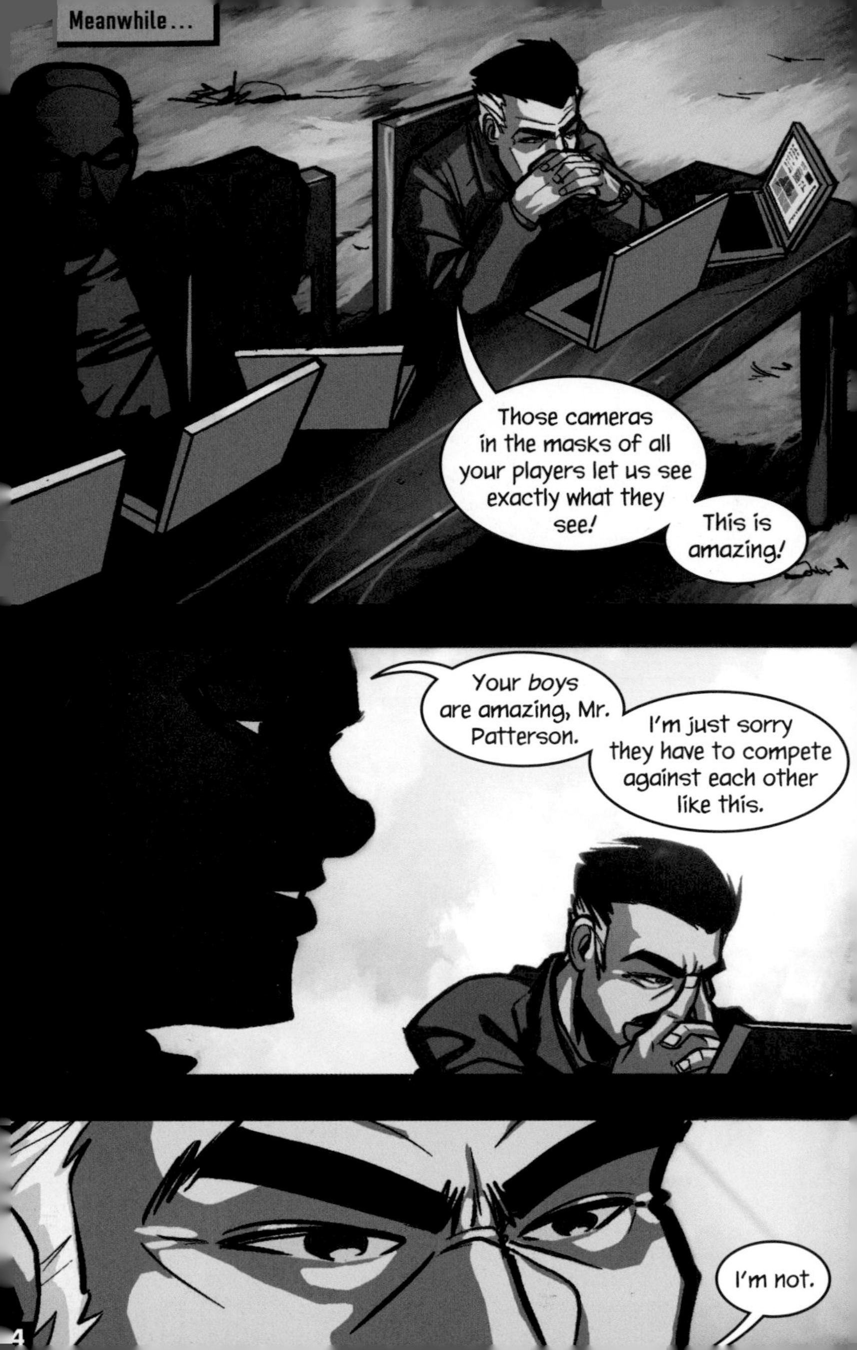

Meanwhile...
Those cameras in the masks of all your players let us see exactly what they see!
This is amazing!
Your *boys* are amazing, Mr. Patterson.
I'm just sorry they have to compete against each other like this.
I'm not.

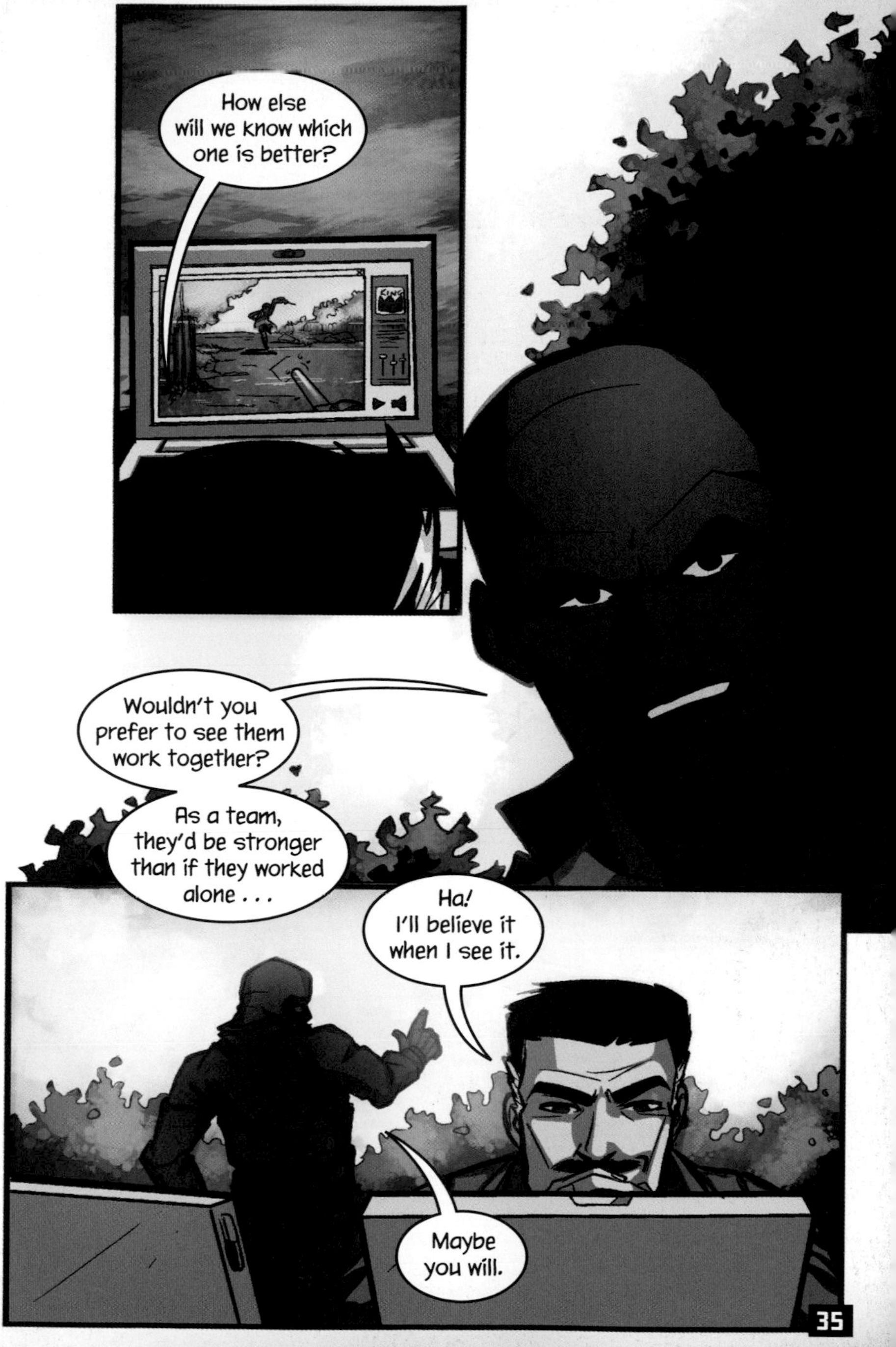
How else will we know which one is better?
Wouldn't you prefer to see them work together?
As a team, they'd be stronger than if they worked alone . . .
Ha! I'll believe it when I see it.
Maybe you will.

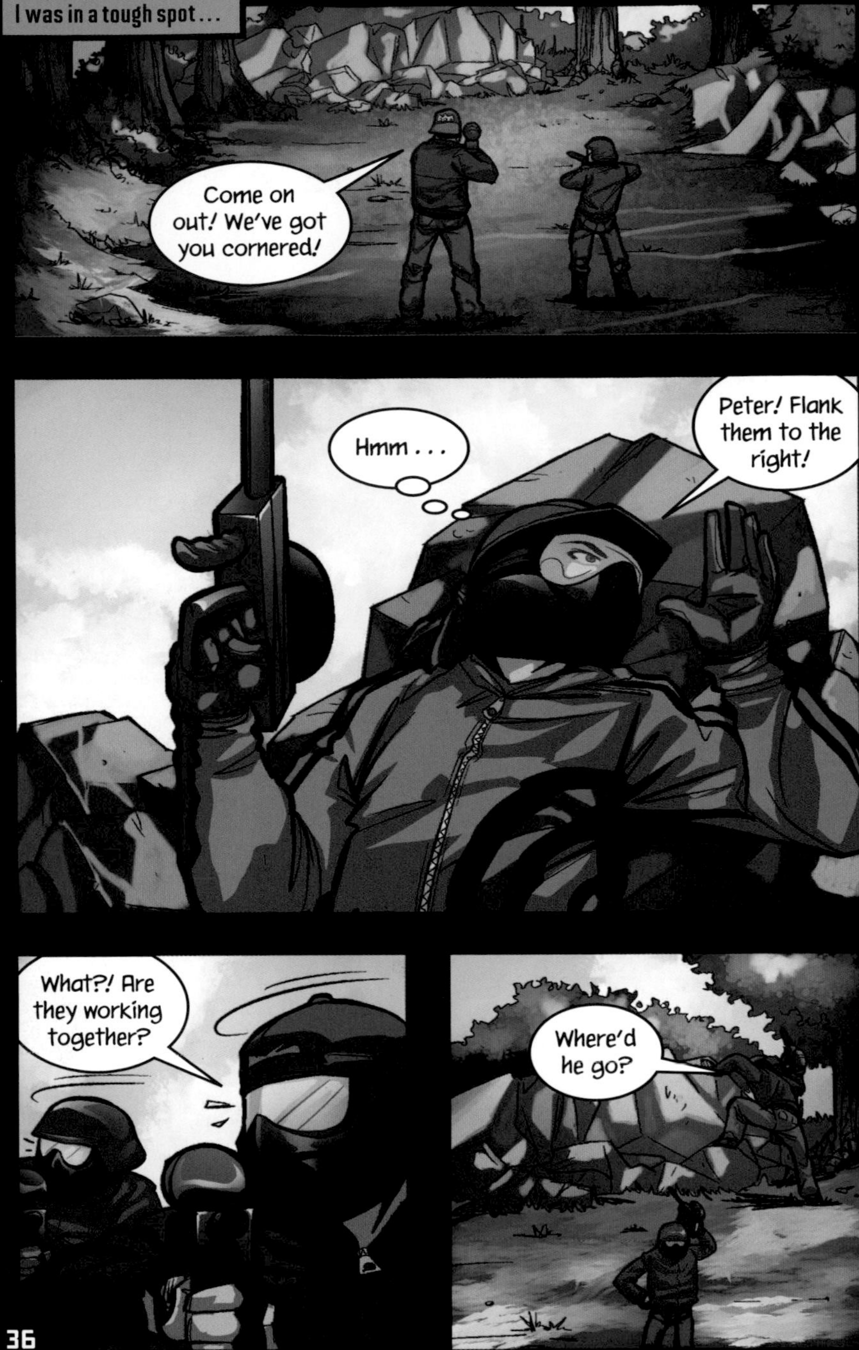

I was in a tough spot . . .
Come on out! We've got you cornered!
Hmm . . .
Peter! Flank them to the right!
What?! Are they working together?
Where'd he go?

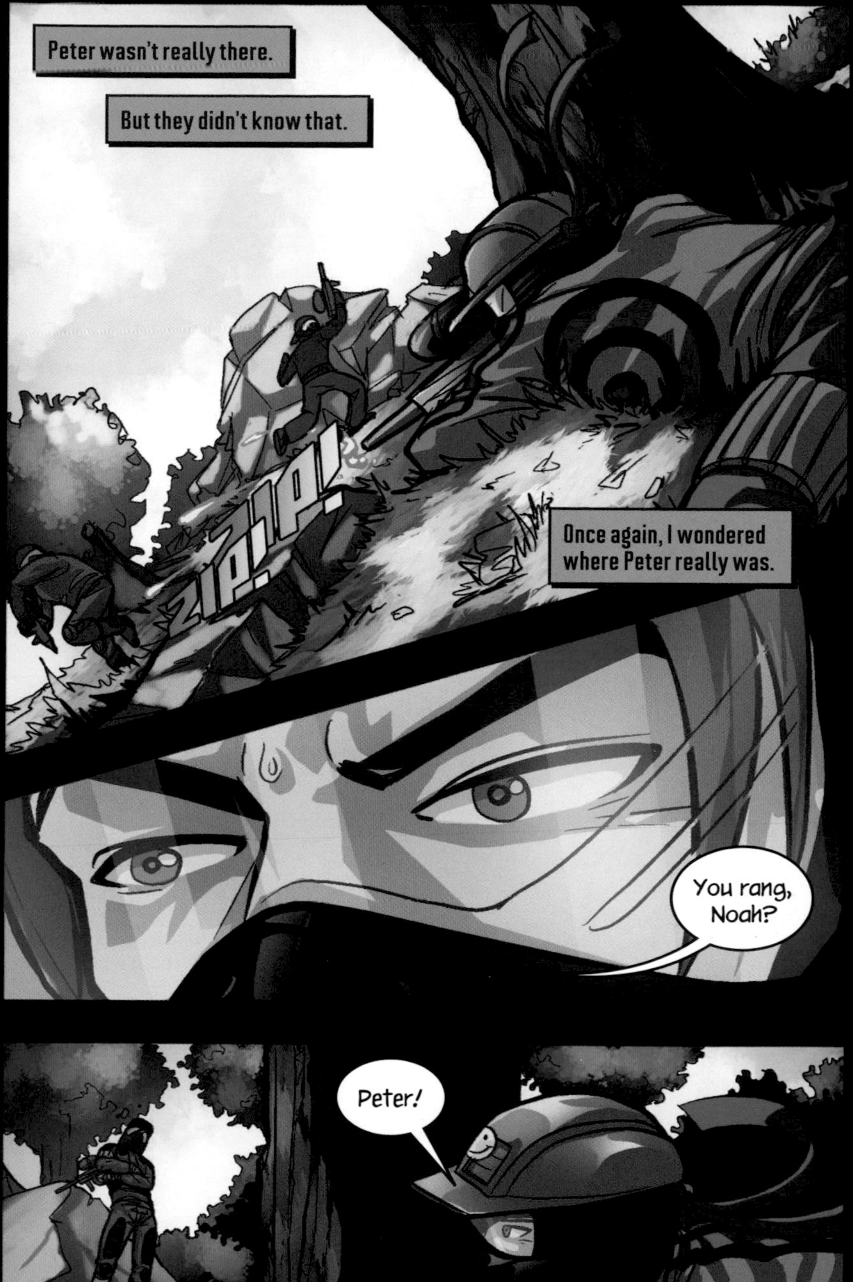
Peter wasn't really there.
But they didn't know that.
ZIP! ZIP!
Once again, I wondered where Peter really was.
You rang, Noah?
Peter!

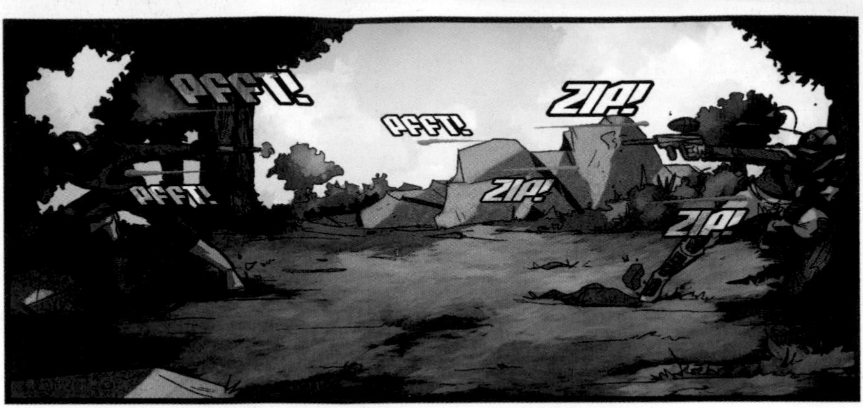
PFFT!
PFFT!
PFFT!
ZIP!
ZIP!
ZIP!

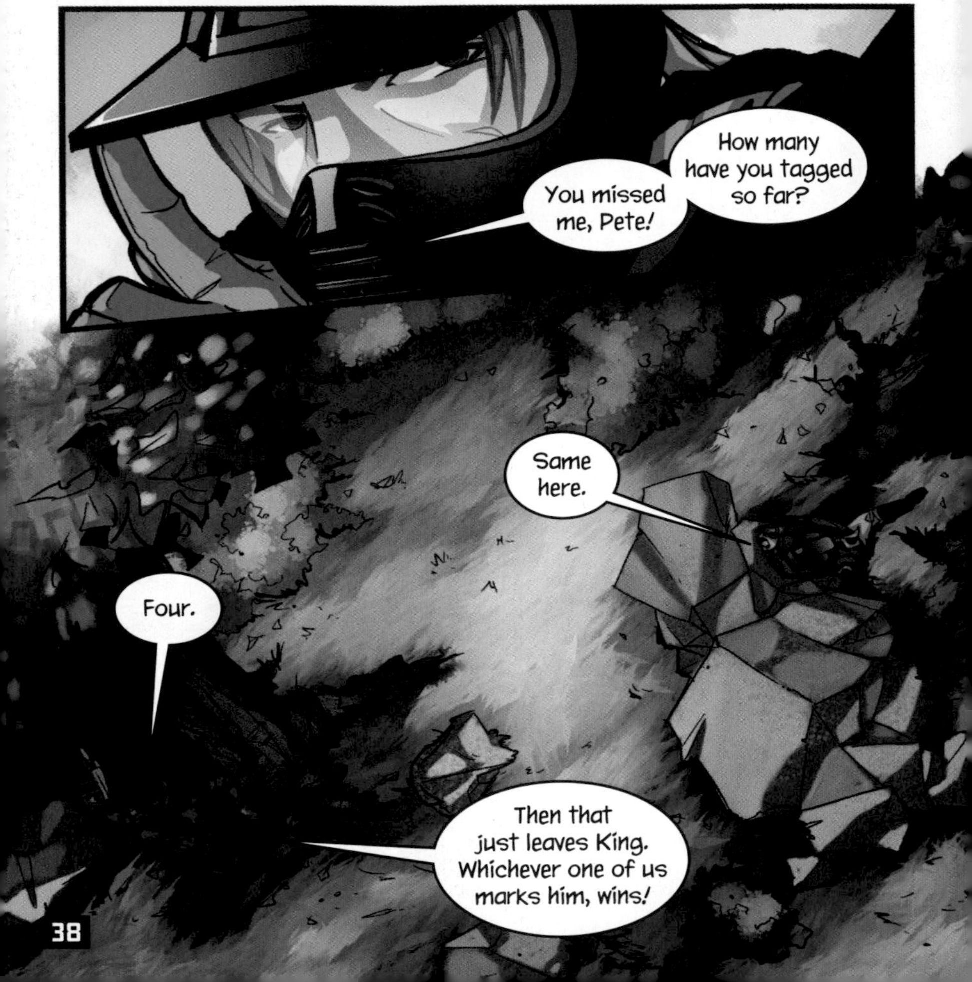
How many have you tagged so far?
You missed me, Pete!
Same here.
Four.
Then that just leaves King. Whichever one of us marks him, wins!

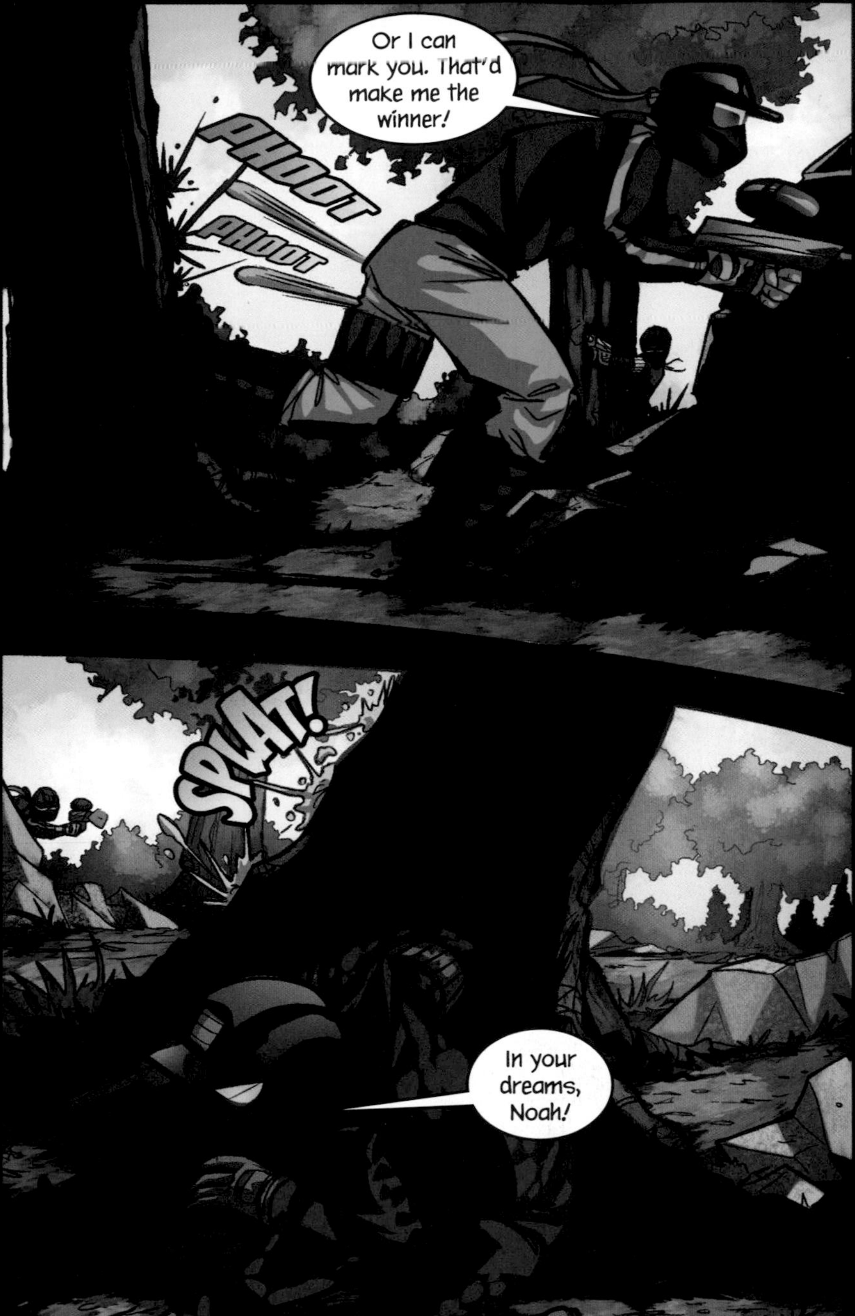
Or I can mark you. That'd make me the winner!
PHOOT
PHOOT
SPLAT!
In your dreams, Noah!

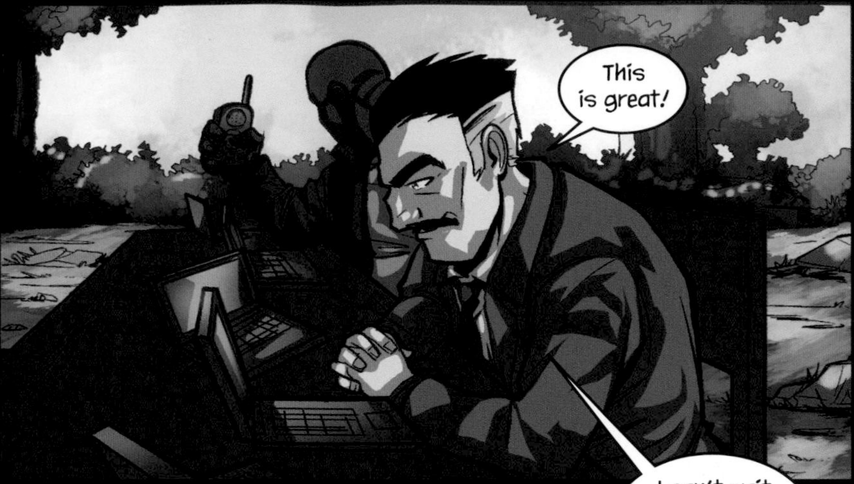
This is great!
I can't wait to see which one of my boys will win!

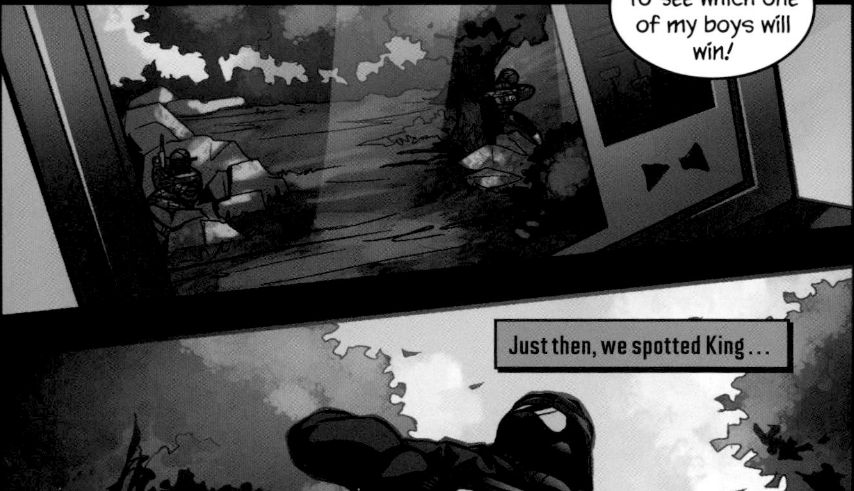

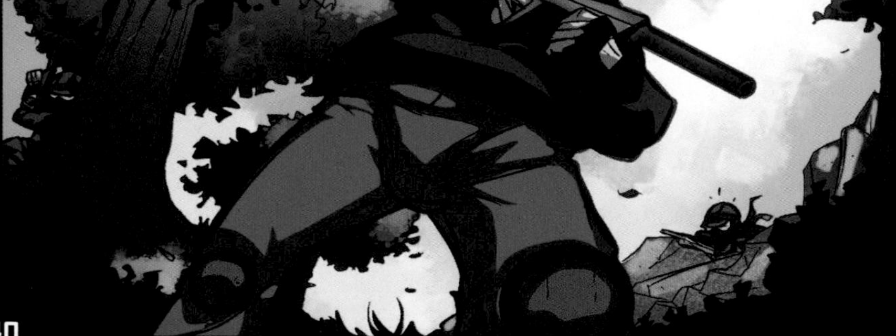
Just then, we spotted King . . .

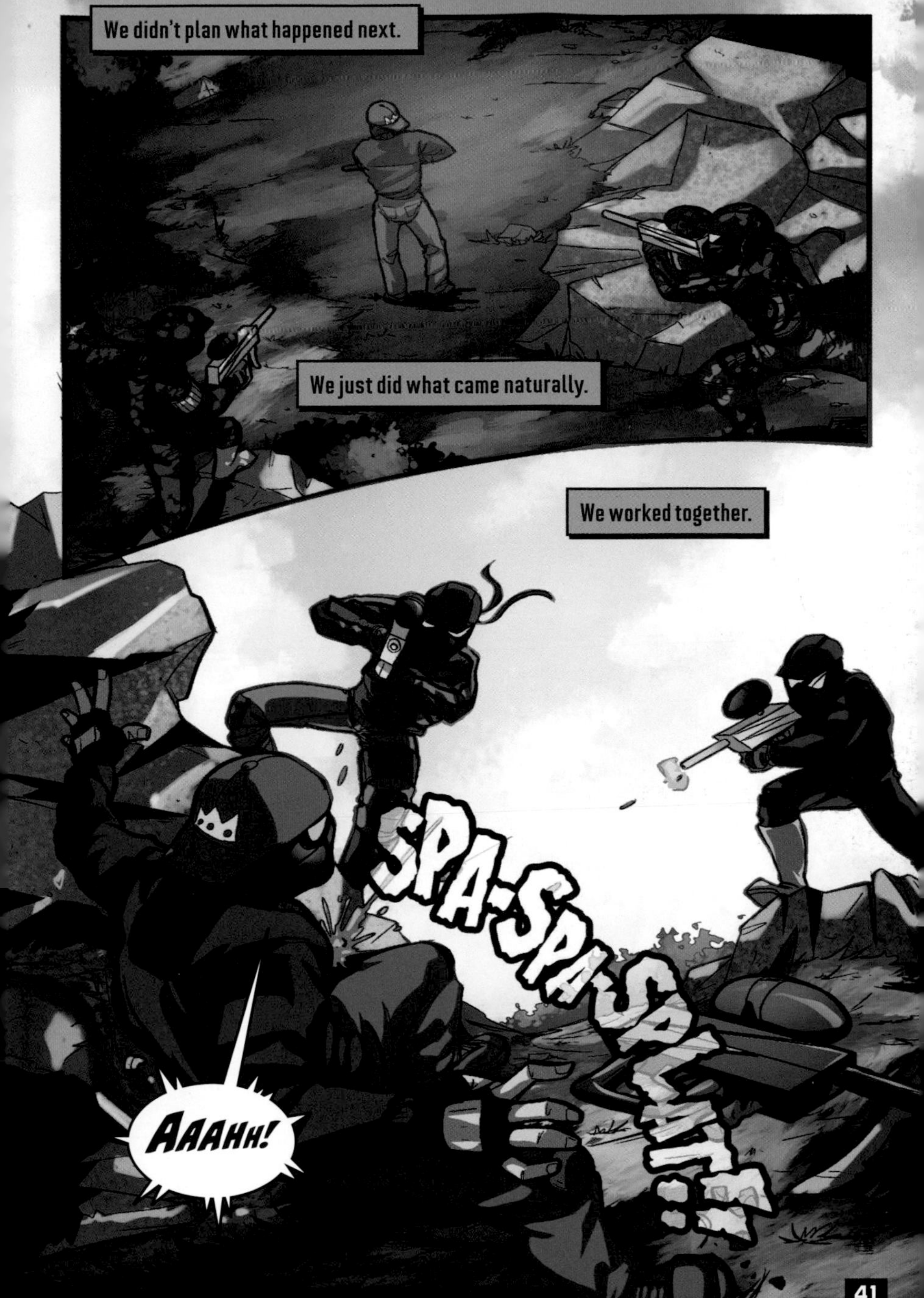
We didn't plan what happened next.
We just did what came naturally.
We worked together.
AAAHH!
SPA-SPA-SPLAT!!

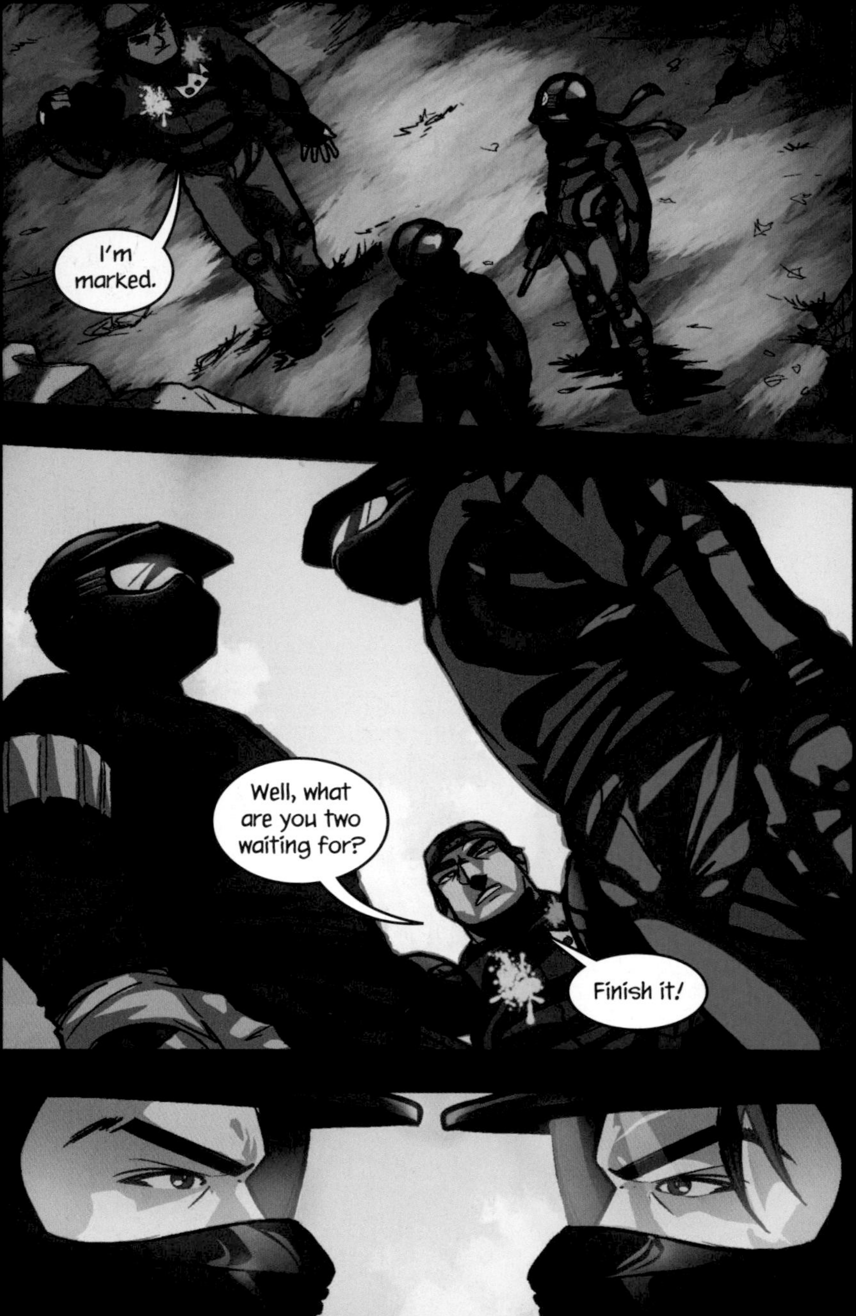
I'm marked.
Well, what are you two waiting for?
Finish it!

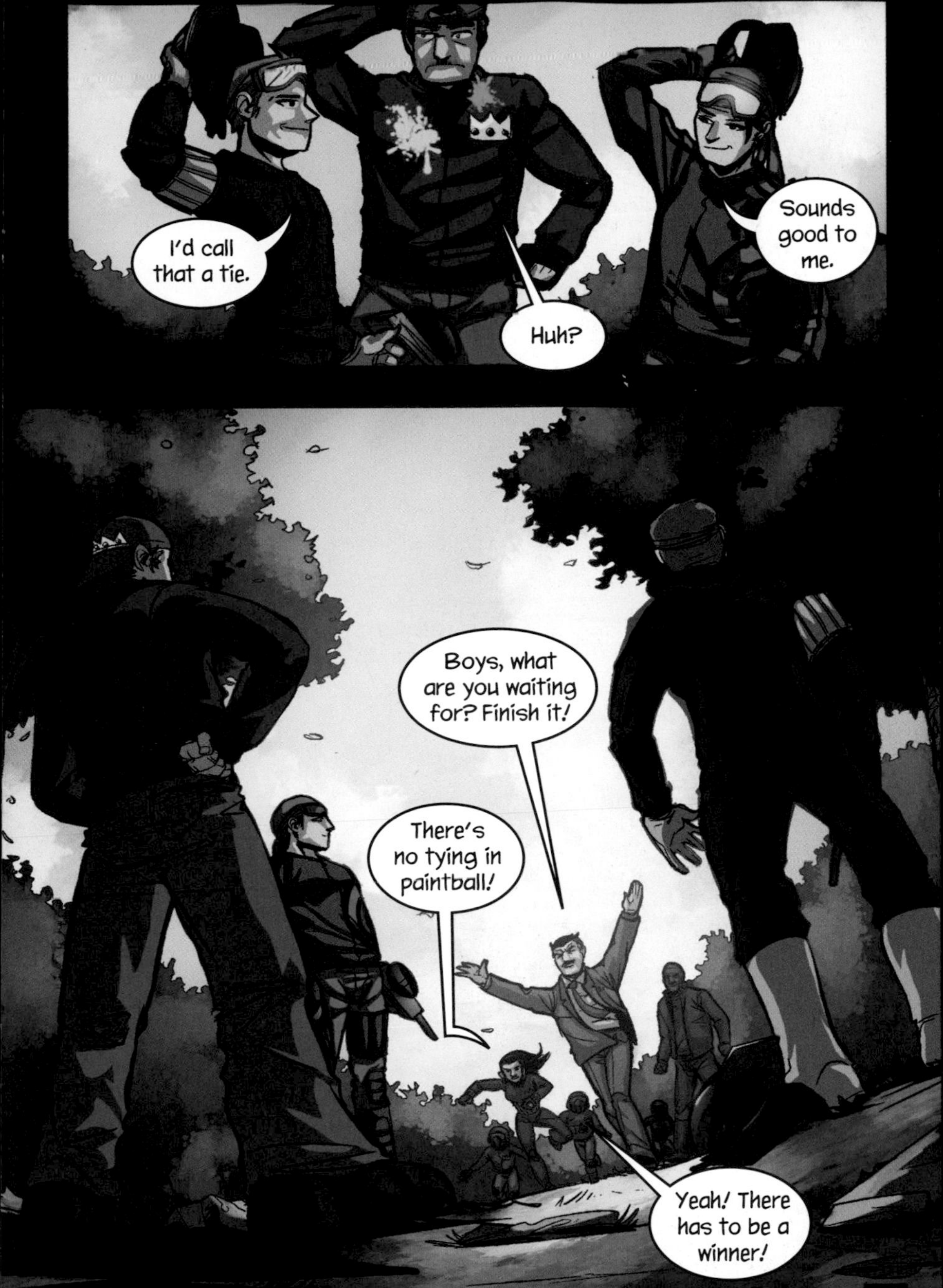
I'd call that a tie.
Huh?
Sounds good to me.
Boys, what are you waiting for? Finish it!
There's no tying in paintball!
Yeah! There has to be a winner!

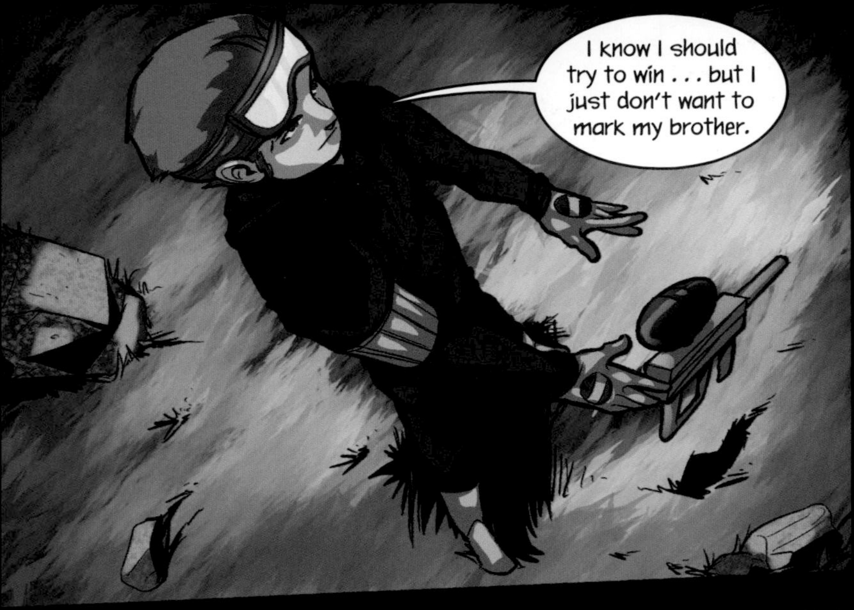
I know I should try to win . . . but I just don't want to mark my brother.

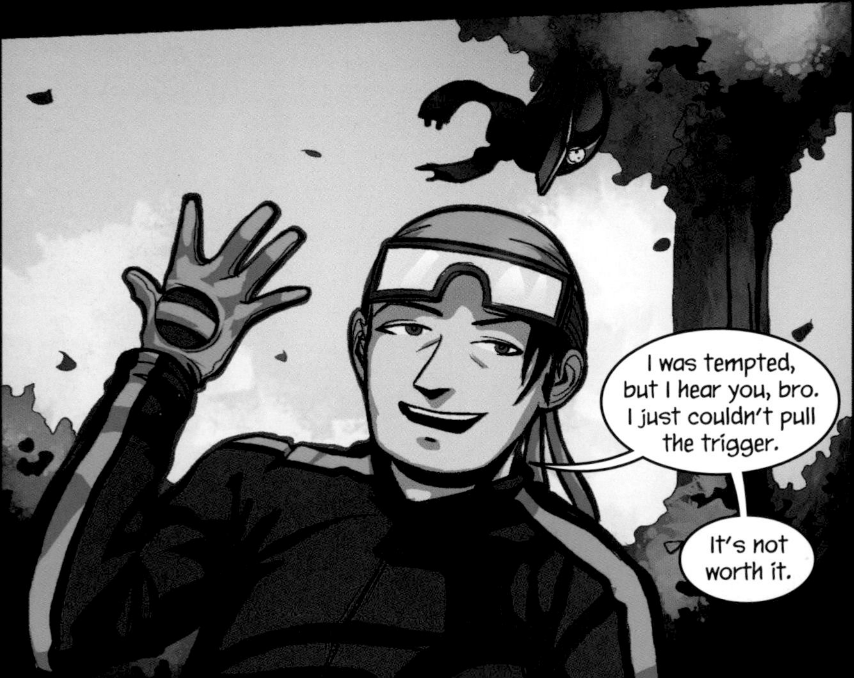
I was tempted, but I hear you, bro. I just couldn't pull the trigger.
It's not worth it.

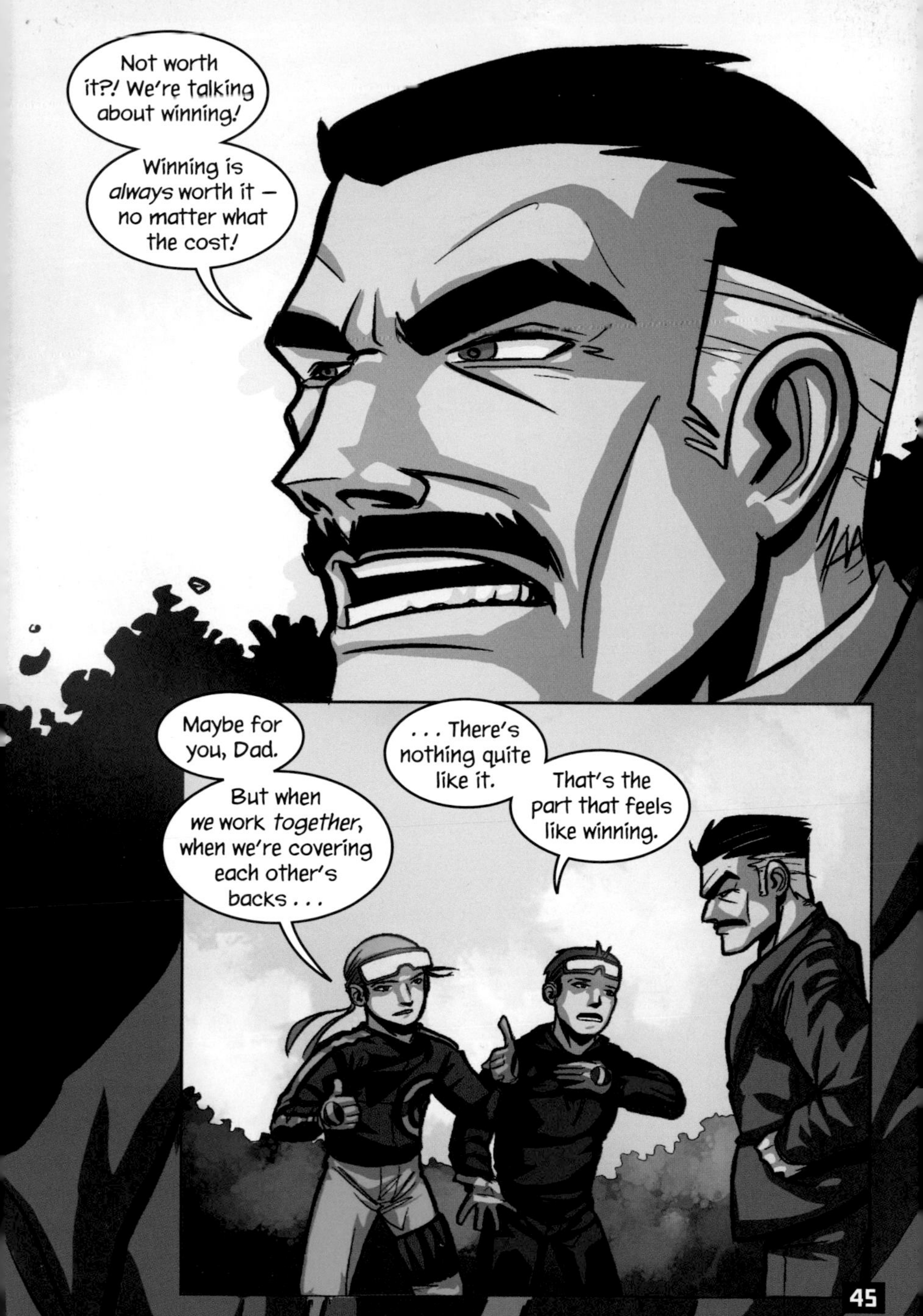
Not worth it?! We're talking about winning!
Winning is *always* worth it — no matter what the cost!
Maybe for you, Dad.
But when we work *together*, when we're covering each other's backs . . .
. . . There's nothing quite like it.
That's the part that feels like winning.

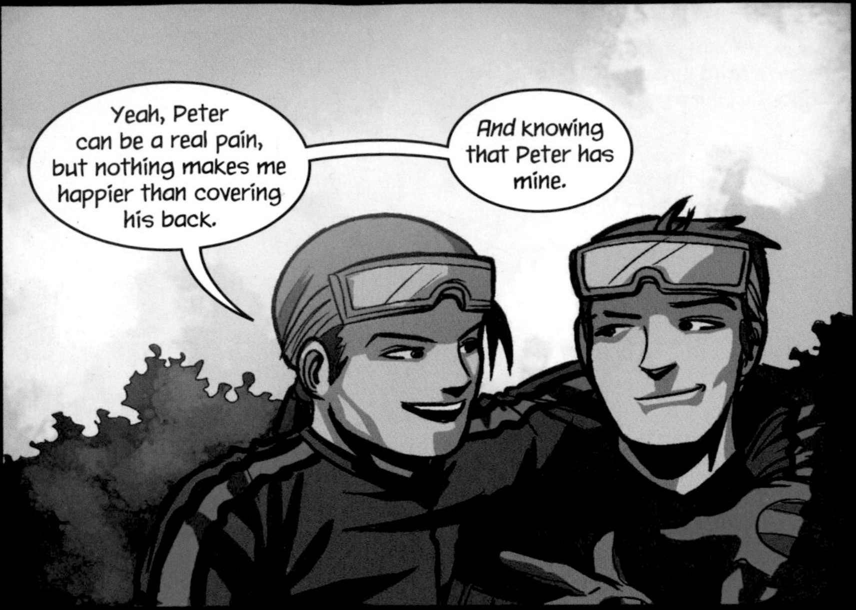
Yeah, Peter can be a real pain, but nothing makes me happier than covering his back.
And knowing that Peter has mine.

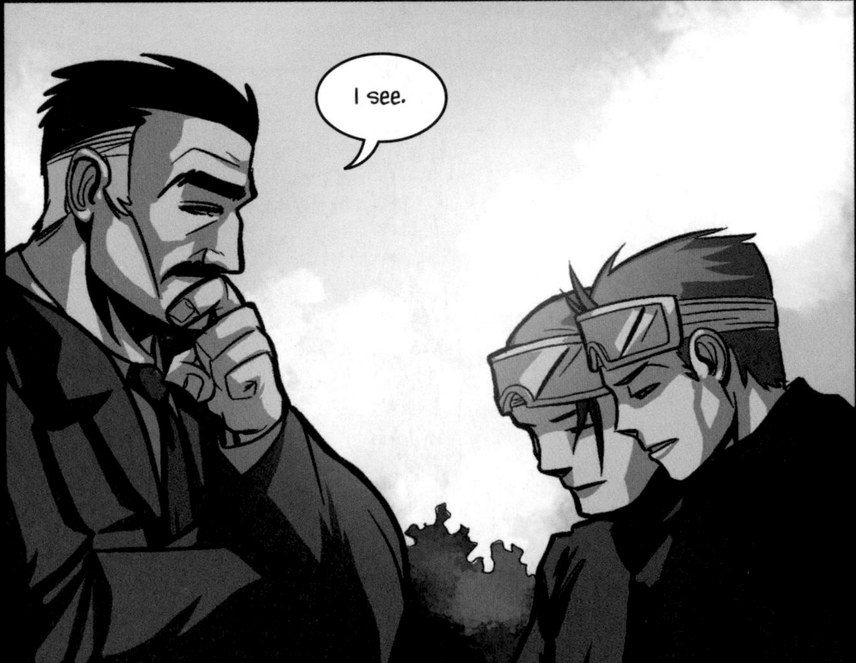
I see.

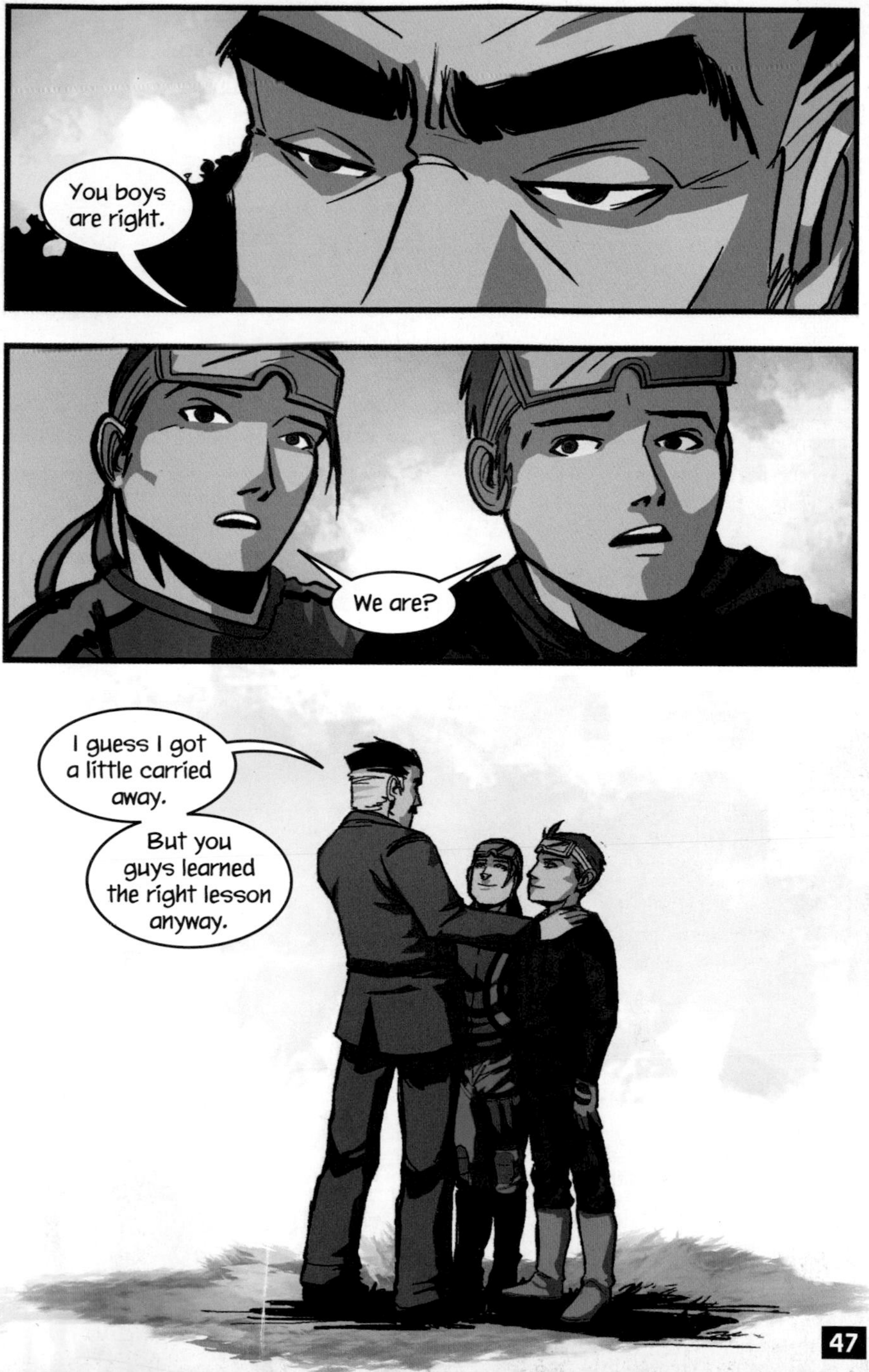
You boys are right.
We are?
I guess I got a little carried away.
But you guys learned the right lesson anyway.

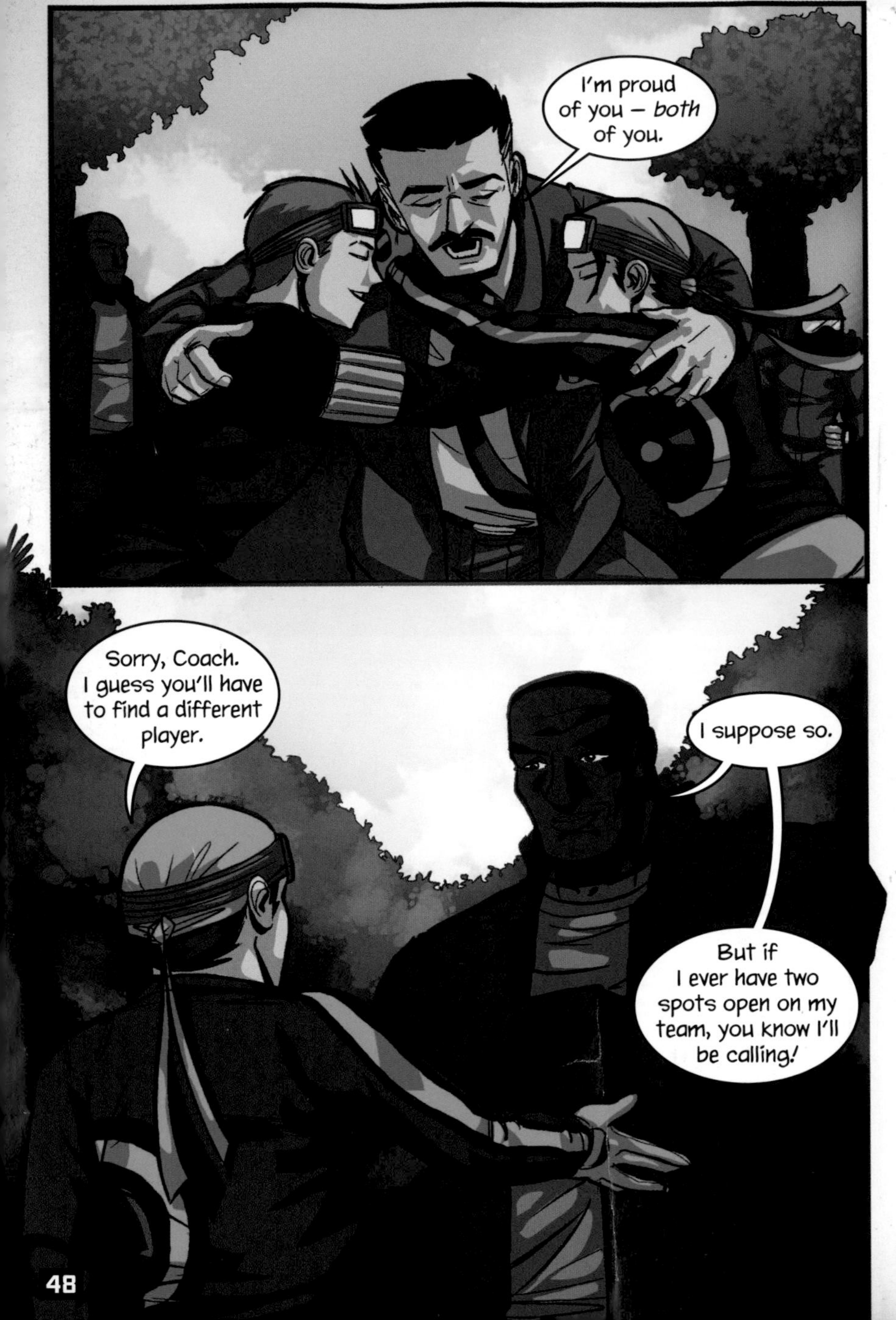
I'm proud of you – *both* of you.
Sorry, Coach. I guess you'll have to find a different player.
I suppose so.
But if I ever have two spots open on my team, you know I'll be calling!

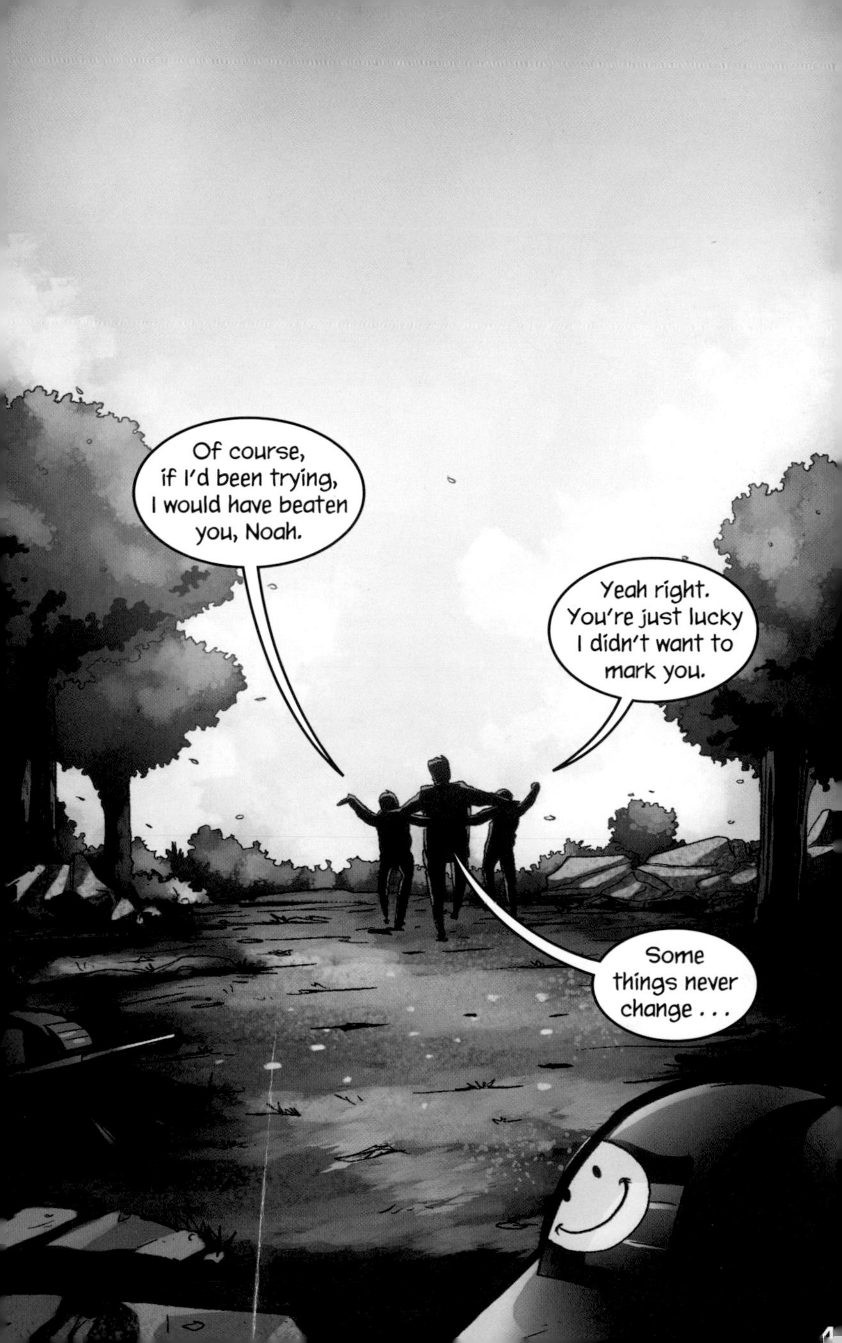
Of course, if I'd been trying, I would have beaten you, Noah.
Yeah right. You're just lucky I didn't want to mark you.
Some things never change . . .

SPORTS ZONE
POSTGAME RECAP

PNT
PAINTBALL

FBL
FOOTBALL

SKT
SKATEBOARDING

BSL
BASEBALL

NOAH

PETER

ECCLESTON TWINS LAY DOWN THEIR MARKERS AND CALL IT A DRAW!

BY THE NUMBERS

FINAL SCORE:
DRAW

POINTS:
NOAH: 5 MARKS
PETER: 5 MARKS

STORY: The heated sibling rivalry in the Royals team tryout came to an unexpected conclusion when both twins readied their markers, took aim, and . . . laid down their arms! The shocking tie forces the Royals to look elsewhere for a new player. Coach Patterson was quoted as saying, "I'm disappointed that one of the Eccleston twins won't be joining our squad, but I'm impressed by their show of brotherhood."

Sports Illustrated KIDS

UP NEXT: SI KIDS INFO CENTER

SZ *POSTGAME EXTRA*

WHERE **YOU** ANALYZE THE GAME!

BLZ vs BKS
3·1
TOR vs ROR
33·32
EAG vs BAN
14·7
SPA vs WLD
4·3
BAN vs WLD
21·15
ROR vs LIG

Today, paintball fans got to see an amazing, action-packed shootout that ended with a surprising twist! Let's go into the stands and ask some fans for their reactions to the contest's shocking conclusion...

DISCUSSION QUESTION 1

When Peter and Noah face off at point-blank range, they call it a draw. Would you have laid down your marker if you were one of them? Why?

DISCUSSION QUESTION 2

Do you think Mr. Eccleston was right when he told his sons that you can't count on anyone but yourself? Discuss your answers.

WRITING PROMPT 1

Peter and Noah are twins. Do you know anyone who is a twin? How would your life be different if you had a twin? Would you want a twin?

WRITING PROMPT 2

Write a short story where Peter AND Noah end up joining the Royals. Are they nervous about playing on television? Do they like their new teammates? Who wins the championship? Write about it.

GLOSSARY

CRUEL (KROO-uhl)—a cruel person deliberately causes pain to others or is happy to see them suffer

IDENTICAL (eye-DEN-ti-kuhl)—exactly alike, as in identical twins

IMPATIENT (im-PAY-shuhnt)—in a hurry and unable to wait, or easily annoyed

LUNATICS (LOO-nuh-tikz)—insane or crazy people

MARKER (MAR-kur)—a marker is the main piece of equipment used in paintball. Markers use expanding gas to shoot paintballs through a barrel.

POINT-BLANK (POINT-BLANGK)—close range

SQUAD (SKWAHD)—a small group of people involved in the same activity, like soldiers in the armed forces, or teammates in a sport

UNFORGIVING (uhn-for-GIV-ing)—not willing to show mercy, or unwilling to forgive mistakes

CREATORS

SCOTT CIENCIN › Author

Scott Ciencin is a *New York Times* bestselling author of children's and adult fiction. He has written comic books, trading cards, video games, and television shows, as well as many non-fiction projects. He lives in Sarasota, Florida with his beloved wife, Denise, and his best buddy, Bear, a golden retriever. He loves writing books for Stone Arch, and is working hard on many more that are still to come.

JESUS ABURTO › Illustrator

Jesus Aburto was born in Monterrey, Mexico. He has been a graphic designer, a colorist, and an illustrator. Aburto has colored popular comic book characters such as Wolverine, Ironman, Blade, and Nightwing. In 2008, Aburto joined Protobunker Studio, where he enjoys working as a full-time comic book illustrator.

FARES MAESE › Colorist

Fares Maese is an illustrator and graphic designer born in Monterrey, Mexico. He currently partners with Ponxlab Studio, where he enjoys working as an illustrator and colorist.

ANDRES ESPARZA › Colorist

Andres Esparza was born in Monterrey, Mexico. Andres has created logos, illustrations, and character designs for several different companies. Andres contributes to a local comic book called *Melanie*, and *PONX* magazine.

BING HAWTIN, TY TAGGART, AND MATTY LYONS IN:

SKATEBOARD SONAR

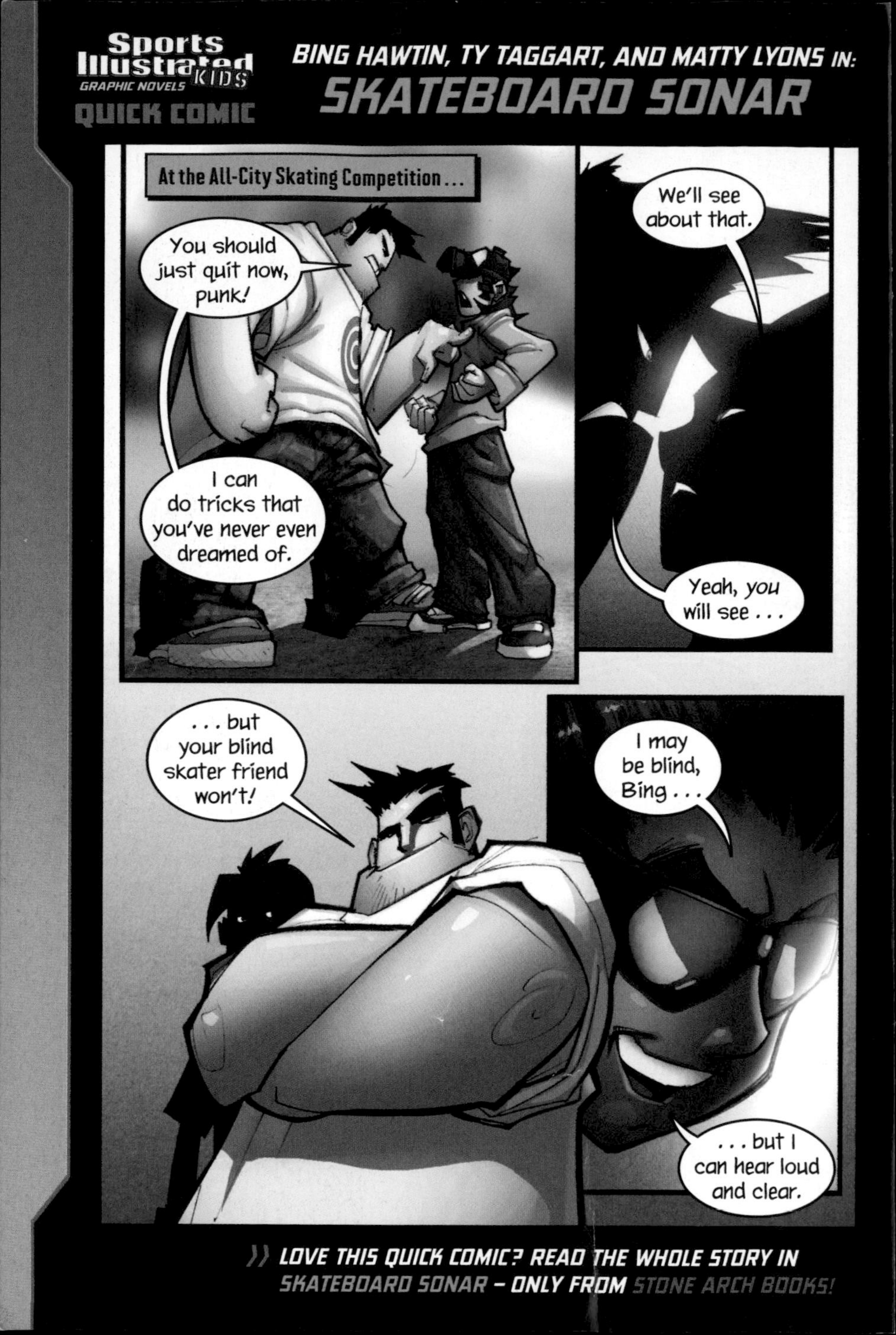
At the All-City Skating Competition . . .
You should just quit now, punk!
I can do tricks that you've never even dreamed of.
We'll see about that.
Yeah, you will see . . .
. . . but your blind skater friend won't!
I may be blind, Bing . . .
. . . but I can hear loud and clear.

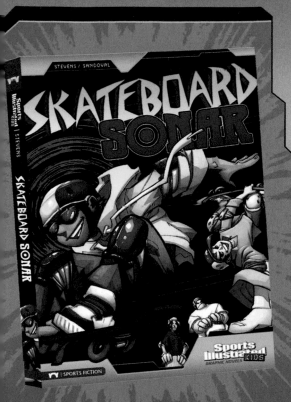

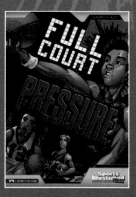